### "Your daughter's a lot like you."

"Well, she's got my hair." Shane smiled.

"Yes, she does." *Dark and silky...*

"And folks say we've got the same eyes."

*With long, black lashes.*

"I believe she has my smile, too, just a little prettier." Shane grinned.

*So handsome...* Rachel watched Shane's mouth soften. Even as she murmured an agreement, Rachel was reliving his kisses, the warmth and sureness of his mouth on hers.

Shane watched the play of emotions over Rachel's face. There was feeling for him in her eyes, and it made him want to kiss her long and slow.

Shane teetered on the edge of that kiss, desire drawing him toward the brink. He had to think of the girls....

Dear Reader,

What a month of wonderful reading Romance has for you! Our FABULOUS FATHERS title, *Most Wanted Dad*, continues Arlene James's miniseries THIS SIDE OF HEAVEN. Single dad and police officer Evans Kincaid can't quite handle his daughter's wild makeup and hairdos. Luckily—or not so luckily—the pretty lady next door is full of advice....

*Do You Take This Child?* is the last book of Marie Ferrarella's THE BABY OF THE MONTH CLUB miniseries—and our BUNDLES OF JOY title. Any-minute-mom-to-be Dr. Sheila Pollack expects to raise her baby all alone. But when the *long-absent* dad-to-be suddenly bursts into the delivery room, Sheila says "I do" between huffs and puffs!

In *Reilly's Bride* by Patricia Thayer, Jenny Murdock moves to Last Hope, Wyoming, to escape becoming a bride. But the town's crawling with eligible bachelors who want wives. So why isn't she happy when she falls for the one man who doesn't want to walk down the aisle?

Carla Cassidy continues THE BAKER BROOD miniseries with *Mom in the Making*. Single dad Russ Blackburn's little son chases away every woman who comes near his dad. It just figures the boy would like Bonnie Baker—a woman without a shred of mother material in her!

And don't miss the handsome drifter who becomes a woman's birthday present in Lauryn Chandler's *Her Very Own Husband*, or the two adorable kids who want their parents together in Robin Nicholas's *Wrangler's Wedding*.

Enjoy!

Melissa Senate,
Senior Editor

Please address questions and book requests to:
Silhouette Reader Service
U.S.: 3010 Walden Ave., P.O. Box 1325, Buffalo, NY 14269
Canadian: P.O. Box 609, Fort Erie, Ont. L2A 5X3

# WRANGLER'S
# WEDDING

## Robin Nicholas

Silhouette
**R O M A N C E™**
Published by Silhouette Books
**America's Publisher of Contemporary Romance**

For
Mom and Dad
One life, one love.

 SILHOUETTE BOOKS

ISBN 0-373-19149-9

WRANGLER'S WEDDING

Copyright © 1996 by Robin Kapala

This edition published by arrangement with Harlequin Books S.A.

® and TM are trademarks of Harlequin Books S.A., used under license.
Trademarks indicated with ® are registered in the United States Patent
and Trademark Office, the Canadian Trade Marks Office and in other
countries.

Printed in U.S.A.

**Books by Robin Nicholas**

Silhouette Romance

*The Cowboy and His Lady* #1017
*Wrangler's Wedding* #1049

---

## ROBIN NICHOLAS

lives in Illinois. She and her husband, Dan, keep busy
raising their son, Nick, and racing harness horses.

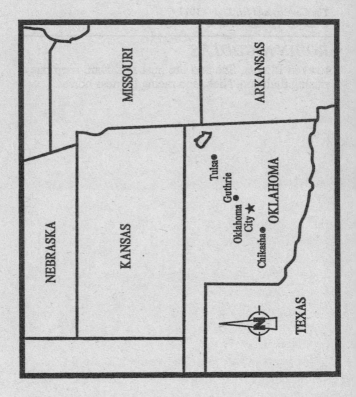

# Chapter One

Rachel Callahan turned from the concession booth and scanned the brightly lit arena grandstand for a splash of red, the color she'd dressed her daughter in for the rodeo at Chickasha tonight. She'd left three-year-old Rose safely settled in the stands with the mother of a barrel-racing friend and that friend's daughter. But Rachel couldn't see a red shirt or the matching ribbon that topped Rose's gold ponytail anywhere.

Her heart began to pound with an age-old fear; a fear recently compounded by her ex-husband's sudden interest in their daughter. Not that Jace Callahan would really resort to child snatching. He didn't have to, with all that Oklahoma oil money behind him, coupled with the clout of belonging to an old ranch family with legal ties. Still, Jace had made repeated threats to take Rose, and right now, it was enough to nudge Rachel into a step of panic.

Then Rachel saw Rose, her golden head bent over her doll, her satin hair ribbon shining under the lights like a red star in the cloudy night sky.

A weakness spread through Rachel, her lungs emptying themselves of a hard-held breath. She stood and stared at that "star," making a fervent wish.

*Keep my baby safe—with me.*

Someone jostled her from behind and Rachel snapped to attention, murmuring an apology as she shifted out of the way. She wanted to go see Rose, but the barrel races were coming up soon. Besides, it was way past Rose's bedtime and if she made an appearance now, Rose might not be willing to let her go.

Rachel sighed. Already, she missed sweet old Lilly Casey. If Lilly hadn't fallen and broken a hip yesterday, Rose would be home in Lilly's care right now, tucked snug in bed with her doll.

Rachel took a long pull of her iced cola, aware of the need to change from the role of mother to competitor, to be mentally primed for her ride. The sale of the horse she'd trained hinged on the gelding's performance tonight. But as she lowered her drink, the sight of a dark-eyed cowboy laughing with a dark-eyed, preteen girl only drove home the desire to hold, and hold on to, her daughter. Rachel watched their matching smiles flash, certain she was looking at father and daughter.

The cowboy turned from the arena fence and the steer-wrestling event going on inside, and bent his head to whisper in the girl's ear, setting her off in a fit of giggles. Rachel was sure she'd seen this cowboy finish out of the money in the calf-roping earlier, although it didn't appear to have affected his mood adversely. He grinned at the girl, who snatched his hat and plopped it on her head, hiding thick bangs and leaving a chocolate-colored ponytail to flow down her slim back. But it was the man who caught Rachel's attention now.

He was one handsome cowboy, drawing the appreciative gaze of more than one cowgirl, herself included. He had smooth-shaven lean features and full lips that had Rachel unconsciously moistening hers. But it was his black hair that had her fingers itching. Cut in a clean edge across the back of his neck, it fell thick, long and shiny on top from a neat side part. He stole back his hat from the girl, raking his hair from his forehead with sun-browned fingers and settling the coal-colored Stetson on his head.

Something about him struck her as familiar. It took only a moment of concentration and Rachel remembered him from another Oklahoma rodeo, two months ago in Guthrie, close to home.

The June night was warm, and Rachel absently rubbed the cold paper cup across her cheek, letting the remaining ice cool her. Except for those striking good looks, she wouldn't have recognized this man as the same cowboy. At Guthrie he'd been on a winning streak, taking not only top money in calf roping, but winning the bull riding, too. And there'd been *women*, not a girl, hanging on his every word, not to mention both arms. He'd caught her notice then, as well, but she'd dismissed him as a typical hell-raising rodeo cowboy.

He wasn't so easy to dismiss tonight. He'd been one hot cowboy at Guthrie, but right now, there was something mighty appealing in the way he smiled despite his hard luck, his attention only on the girl.

They broke into another round of laughter and Rachel's responding smile was wistful. For all Jace's threats to take custody, the man had trouble remembering the date of his daughter's birthday. Rachel watched the cowboy with his daughter, certain Rose would never know that kind of closeness with her father, no matter what Jace did.

A sigh was slipping past Rachel's lips when the cowboy ruffled the girl's bangs and glanced over, meeting her gaze straight on. For a moment the piercing eyes held her, then he smoothed his hand gently over the girl's hair as if he'd somehow read Rachel's thoughts and shared in her feelings. Rachel softened in response to his understanding.

Something flickered in the cowboy's eyes, a spark of male approval lighting his gaze, which remained straightforward and unapologetic. Rachel lowered the cup from her now cold cheek and squashed it in her hand. The last thing she needed was for some cowboy to think she was coming on to him.

Rachel tossed her cup into a nearby trash can and turned away, heading for the barn where she'd left her horse. Her dust-kicking stride stirred a breeze across her face even as it caused sweat to trickle from beneath her hat brim and down her temples. Her hair, long and gold like Rose's, hung hot and heavy against her back. Wrapping it into a neat bun at her nape would have felt cooler, but there was no time to be fussing with it now, just as there was no time to be dallying over handsome cowboys or cussing no-good fathers.

She had a horse to sell; a prospective buyer in the stands waiting to see if the sorrel gelding she'd trained would suit his daughter.

When her turn came, Rachel was ready. Spurred on by the nearly depleted checkbook she'd placed earlier under her truck seat, Rachel curled the sorrel around the barrels like stripes around a candy cane, the fringe on her red shirt flying, matching feathers fluttering in her hatband as horse and woman ran the cloverleaf pattern in winning time.

When it was all over, Rachel collected Rose and headed for her handkerchief-of-a-ranch west of Guthrie, with an empty horse trailer and hope in her heart that she could hang on to the place, after all.

The interstate linking Chickasha to Oklahoma City was late-night quiet and it seemed a long time before Rachel hit the state route and, finally, the turnoff that led to the Callahan ranch. Rose had slept the whole way, chubby hands slack on the doll in her lap, leaving Rachel to envy the innocent oblivion only a child can know. Rachel's mind churned with worry over the fact that she couldn't train horses until she found someone to replace Lilly.

Rachel rubbed her eyes, a glance in the rearview mirror revealing blue irises rimmed with red from fatigue. A light mist had begun to fall and she was glad home was just two miles ahead as the road took on a polished slickness. Rachel willed her mind free of her troubles, only to find it filled with the image of a dark-eyed cowboy with shiny black hair.

She hadn't meant to give that man another thought. But she couldn't lose the picture in her mind of him laughing with his daughter. His name came to her then, as if falling with the rain before her eyes. Shane Purcell, the rodeo announcer had called him. Rachel recalled both rodeos at which she had seen him. He'd seemed such a different man each time and she couldn't help wondering which was the real Shane Purcell....

Flashing lights ahead, just off the other side of the road, caught her attention, Rachel slowed her pickup automatically, her senses on alert. Rose stirred, and Rachel cast her daughter a concerned glance, relieved when the child seemed to drift into deep sleep again. Her relief was short-lived when she saw a truck and two-horse trailer in the shadows, the rig half in and half out of the ditch, the bumper of the truck folded around the unyielding trunk of a tree.

Rachel eased her pickup onto the shoulder. Across the road, the truck was nose down into the ditch, the trailer jackknifed, but at least upright. She heard a horse inside it calling shrilly, shifting restlessly, but not thrashing around. Rachel thought the horse might be all right, but dread twisted in her stomach at what shape the driver and passengers in the crumpled truck might be.

Taking a flashlight from the glove compartment, Rachel hesitated, considering Rose. She didn't want to leave her daughter alone in the pickup. What if a car came along? Her rig was barely off the road and could easily be struck. Who knew what kind of stranger might stop? And who knew what kind of person might be in that truck over there right now?

She ought to just drive on home and call for help. But even as the thought crossed her mind, she shut off the pickup's engine and set the emergency brake. When Rachel was eight, her mother had died in an auto crash. She couldn't leave, knowing someone's life might depend on her immediate help.

Switching on the dim overhead light so she could see Rose, Rachel let herself out the door. Rose slept on and Rachel ran across the road, not giving herself time to think before she scrambled down the ditch and shone her light through the truck's window on the lone occupant.

It was the cowboy. Shane Purcell.

He must have driven up from Chickasha through Guthrie, Rachel thought, shivering despite the warm night, the mist dampening her hair and clothes. Shane was sprawled back in the seat, his hat slightly askew, blood trickling from above his left eye, his right forearm twisted in an awkward manner. He was unconscious, but she saw the faint rise and fall of his chest.

Rachel thought suddenly of his daughter. Had she been in the truck, too? Had she gone for help?

Shaky hand slipping on the wet handle, Rachel opened the door, surprised when the dome light came on. Shane was wearing a seat belt and, considering the accordion fold of the front end of the truck and the cracked windshield, she suspected he'd just become one of the lucky statistics known as survivors. His tanned skin had an underlying pallor. She debated removing his hat, but thought better; it might be stanching the flow of blood from his wound. Afraid to move him in any way, not wanting to jar his arm and uncertain as to the full extent of his injuries, Rachel simply laid a hand on his chest, feeling his heartbeat, her pulse calming at its steady rhythm.

Rachel caught her lip, wondering what to do, when Shane moaned, his eyes opening in heavy blinks until they focused on her. Still leaning close, she saw in his gaze a confusion, which slowly gave way to a glimmer of recognition and then a glaze of pain before his eyes drifted closed again.

Curling her fist in concerned frustration, Rachel started to pull away. Shane clasped his hand about her wrist and she drew nearer.

His lips parted, his words coming as if pushing their way through great pain. "My horse—"

"Shh," Rachel soothed, thinking the girl must not have been with him if he'd asked about the horse. Still, she needed to be sure. "I think the horse is fine, but what about your daughter? Was she with you when you crashed?"

"Laura's...home. Guthrie..." he managed to say, much to Rachel's relief, but then he was gone again, his grasp loosening, his hand falling limply. Rachel was both grateful for the unconscious state that spared him from pain, and frightened by it.

She searched her mind for a course to follow, forgetting the horse for a moment. Leaving Shane here while she went for help seemed the only answer, until she spotted the cellular phone on the seat near Shane's leg.

In that same moment Rachel heard the wail of a siren. She straightened. From the direction of the ranch, and of Guthrie and the hospital there, beacons of light whirled in the darkness. Her heart lifted with hope. Maybe Shane had called for help before he blacked out. Rachel touched a hand to Shane's pale cheek, then backed away, closing the door to keep out the drizzling rain.

The sirens had not yet awakened Rose, and Rachel dashed to the back of the trailer to check on the horse. She wasn't fooled by the nondescript brown gelding that swung its head to greet her. She knew a good roping horse was worth tens of thousands of dollars.

The gelding didn't appear scraped up too badly, all things considered, but the gash on its right shoulder worried Rachel, for blood had formed a small pool at its hoof.

The horse gave a rumbling nicker and Rachel spoke quietly to it. Like a typical cowboy, Shane seemed more concerned about his horse than his injuries. She couldn't help worrying herself what would become of the gelding once help arrived.

The ambulance and a trooper's car were drawing near. Rachel hurried to her truck where Rose was rubbing still-closed eyes. She stood outside, waiting and ready to flag down help if need be, when the sirens let up, leaving only arcs of light cutting through the darkness as both vehicles slowed and stopped.

At Rose's first whimper, Rachel opened the truck door and slid inside, setting aside the flashlight to gather her child in her arms. Rose nestled heavy and warm against her shoulder and fell back asleep.

Rachel was sitting there when a burly trooper approached her.

"You happen to know that injured cowboy, Ma'am?"

Rachel hesitated, something inside her wanting to give an unequivocal yes, while at the same time, wariness held the word back, simultaneous pictures flashing in her mind of Shane with his daughter, and Shane with the women at Guthrie. "I've seen him at a couple rodeos," she finally answered, "but I don't know him."

She gave the trooper what information she could, watching over his shoulder as the paramedics went to work. Before going to check on Shane's condition, the trooper confirmed in a friendly drawl that Shane had indeed called in for his own rescue.

Rachel tucked Rose back into the car seat, shutting the door and turning as Shane was lifted into the ambulance on a stretcher, an IV hooked up to his arm. They'd taken off his hat and he looked somehow vulnerable without it, a thick patch of white gauze at his temple contrasting with his dark hair. Some protective instinct filled her with a need to go with him.

But of course, she couldn't. The ambulance fled down the road and Rachel waited anxiously as the trooper approached.

"Pretty tough cowboy."

"Will he be all right?"

"He's conscious. He's likely got a concussion and he's for sure got a broken arm." The trooper eyed her horse trailer with undisguised hope. "He was worried as hell—heck—about his horse. Says he lives alone in Nebraska. Any chance you know some place around here to take it?"

The trooper seemed relieved when she volunteered to take responsibility for the horse, helping her unload the gelding from Shane's trailer and into her own.

A short time later she had Shane's horse settled in a stall. While Rose slept on, Rachel cleaned up the gelding as best she could, then ended up putting in a call to the vet about the gash on its shoulder. Doc

Winslow came out and stitched up the horse; all the while, Rachel's thoughts kept turning to Shane and his injuries.

It was almost four in the morning before Rachel tucked Rose into bed in the small ranch-style house she'd grown up in. She watched guiltily as her daughter stretched ballerina-like, pointing small toes as if relieved, even in sleep, to be free of the car seat. Rachel couldn't help thinking how it could have been her and Rose in that ditch.

Bone weary, Rachel showered, checking on Rose once more before she went down the hall to the kitchen and put in a call to the hospital. The nurse there seemed determined to protect Shane's privacy. Rachel explained who she was, but since she wasn't "family," the most she could get out of the woman was "satisfactory condition." Frustrated, Rachel reminded herself that the nurse was only following policy. But she exacted a promise from the woman to let Shane know his horse was being cared for, and that she would be in touch.

Pushing her damp hair over her shoulder, Rachel sat at the kitchen table in her summer nightgown and looked out the window. The rain had let up and the light of false dawn shone on the horizon. Although she stared outside, Rachel wasn't oblivious to the envelopes of bills lying next to the sugar bowl.

She shoved a hand through her bangs, her eyes drifting shut. Shane's face flashed behind her closed lids and she realized she couldn't wait for the morn-

ing, when she could get her chores done and go see
how he was. She ought to be worrying instead about
whether he'd pay the bill she'd run up with Doc
Winslow. It was probably only the fact that she'd seen
Shane with his daughter, then come across him, hurt
and alone, that drew her to him so strongly. Better to
remember the other Shane Purcell—the one from the
Guthrie rodeo, with women clinging to both arms.

On that wise note, Rachel went to bed, only to
dream of the dark-eyed cowboy.

"Very well, then, Mr. Purcell. Take your own bath.
But let me warn you, Dr. Martin will be very upset
with you if you get your cast or stitches wet."

With that, the nurse turned away in a huff. Shane
glared at her broad shoulders as she swept through the
door. He'd probably catch hell from the doctor for
giving the woman a hard time, but damned if he cared.
Right now, busted up and down on his luck, he didn't
need the added humiliation of some strange woman
treating him like an overgrown boy.

Half an hour later, after an unauthorized trip to the
bathroom that left his head reeling and a sponge bath
that dampened the sheets and his sling, Shane lay back
a moment, realizing he couldn't tie his hospital gown
back on. It was a hell of thing to sleep in, anyway,
twisting and balling up every time he moved.

The bed was cranked to a sitting position and Shane
rested his head on the pillow, flipping the top sheet
over his legs and ignoring the damp bottom sheet

against his bare back. He wondered what was keeping Doc Martin. He'd expected the doctor to come by and release him by now. He'd expected the woman from the rodeo to show up, as well, with word on his horse.

Shane was worried about Cash. But somehow, he wasn't worried that Cash wasn't being taken care of. Rachel Callahan had been pure cowgirl from her boot heels up and she'd shown she knew her way around a horse. Although he hadn't competed in the last bull-riding event, Shane had lingered for the barrel races, as much for himself as for Laura, who was showing an interest in the sport. He'd watched the woman compete, and while he wasn't really good with names, he'd committed Rachel's to memory when it was announced.

She'd been something in her red shirt and pants, her angel-gold hair flying under the lights. He'd liked the way her horse worked; liked the flicker of its ears before the run, a sign the gelding had been ready and waiting for the rider's cue. Barrel racers generally trained their own horses and in this woman's case, it was to her credit.

Just before he'd wrapped his truck around that tree, he'd given some thought to Rachel. He hadn't recognized her as a regular on the circuit, but he was certain he'd seen her at some other rodeo. She'd been alone last night and wasn't wearing any rings on her fingers—he'd checked when he'd caught her watching him. Not that she'd been inviting anything with that almost-melancholy look in her eyes. But that sad gaze had touched a chord in him, as though they'd somehow connected on a higher plane.

Shane sighed, thinking that was a foolish notion. He hadn't been able to "connect" with the woman he'd married and had a child with, let alone with a woman he didn't know. But even as he scoffed at the idea, Shane was thankful fate had dropped his horse into Rachel's barn and left him with the opportunity to get acquainted.

With that thought on his mind, Shane sat up and slipped off his sling, reaching for the hospital gown pooled in his lap. The sound of a softly drawn breath pulled his gaze toward the door.

Rachel. Shane stilled, entranced by lustrous blue eyes trained on his chest and full lips forming a perfect O. Even as his mind was cataloging the creamy complexion and the willowy figure in a flowing blue-flowered dress, it was warning him that Rachel looked much younger than she had from a distance last night. He was thirty-two. In the morning light, Rachel didn't look a day over eighteen.

Shane shoved his good arm into a sleeve and shrugged the gown onto his shoulder, aware Rachel's eyes followed the movement. He slid the other sleeve over his cast and tried to cover that shoulder but the gown slithered back down. Shane made a sound of disgust. His bare chest might have gotten Rachel's attention, but his awkwardness probably wasn't making much of an impression. "Think you could give me a hand, Rachel?"

"I— Of course." She peered out the doorway toward the nurses' station as if checking to see if someone was watching, then she crossed the room to his bedside. The skirt of her dress swirled about her slim legs and the white sandals strapped daintily about her slender ankles scuffed lightly on the polished floor. Rachel was even prettier close up, with long dark lashes and pearl-white teeth that caught nervously at her bottom lip. Shane added a couple more years to her age, feeling a little better about the attraction he felt for her.

Careful to keep his back to the mattress, Shane pulled up the gown again. "Just tie it off, if you will."

Setting her small white purse at the foot of the bed, Rachel took hold of the ties with long slim fingers that looked more apt to play piano keys than grasp leather reins. Her hair fell over her shoulders as she leaned to tie the strings at the base of his neck and Shane sucked in a breath when the silky strands teased his chest through the thin hospital gown. The fresh clean scent of her wrapped around him as her arms wound about his neck. Her dress had a scoop neck that dipped just low enough to set his imagination running. It was almost a relief when she moved away.

"Thanks." Shane hung the sling back around his neck and tucked in his injured arm.

"You're welcome." Rachel picked up her purse and clutched it to her middle. Shane noticed her knuckles were white. Her gaze darted to the door before she asked, "How are you feeling, Mr. Purcell?"

Mr. Purcell. Now that did make him feel old. And it gave him the feeling she was trying to put some distance between them. She had a soft round drawl capable of wrapping a man around her finger, and the most appealing part of all was that she seemed oblivious to the fact.

"I feel like I rode a bull last night, after all," Shane teased, but he gave her a direct look, letting her know that all her attempts to keep a distance were to no avail. "Just call me Shane."

Rachel stared right back at him as if to say she'd put that distance there to stay. Shane went on, undaunted: "I want to thank you for stopping last night. The trooper came by to tell me you took my horse home and the nurse gave me your message. It's helped knowing he was in good hands."

That brought her a step closer, but not for any reason he might have hoped. "I had to get the vet out for your horse last night."

"What's wrong with Cash?" Shane straightened, the movement hurting his head, her blue eyes and soft drawl forgotten as his mind switched gears to his horse. He distinctly remembered Rachel telling him last night that the horse was fine. But he didn't say so, aware of the defensive look that came over her face.

"He has a gash on his shoulder. Doc Winslow sewed him up but he was fussing with the stitches this morning. Doc said if he won't let them be, the cut will just have to heal on its own.''

*Damn.* ''How many stitches?''

''Twelve.''

Twelve. That was a pretty deep cut. And on a shoulder. Every movement would disturb the wound, slow the healing. *Damn.* Shane threaded his hand through his hair. But noting the rigid set to Rachel's shoulders, he made a point of saying, ''I guess I owe you more thanks than I thought.''

She seemed to relent a little. ''I'm real sorry.''

Rachel sounded sincere, the drawl getting to Shane again. ''Things could be worse,'' he assured her. ''At least Laura was already home when the accident happened.''

Shane braced himself then, expecting some question about his daughter living in Guthrie, a fact he remembered telling Rachel. That would naturally lead to him explaining that his daughter didn't live with him, that he'd lost custody of his child through divorce.

Usually when he was with Laura, Shane gave women a wide berth. His time with Laura was for Laura alone, and their family history was nobody's business but their own. Even now, Shane bristled, regretting he'd brought up Laura's name, expecting the usual barrage of personal questions.

But Rachel merely nodded, her glance darting to the door again. It occurred to Shane that she might have someone waiting out there and suddenly he was struggling not to ask some personal questions himself. Then Rachel asked, "How did the accident happen?"

"Tire blew out. Next thing I knew, the trailer was pushing me right for the ditch."

Rachel murmured sympathetically. She might well have purred in his ear, the way it set his pulse drumming. She hitched her purse strap onto her shoulder as if she was getting ready to leave and belatedly Shane said, "Won't you sit down?"

"I'm sorry, I can't stay."

He could believe it, the way she watched the door as if she expected whoever was waiting to come and pluck her out of the room.

"I would like to know what the doctors say about your fractured arm," Rachel added. "I understand you probably have a concussion, too."

"I do, but it's not the first time and I've got a pretty hard head." Shane grinned, but the grin faded when he spoke of his arm. His rope-throwing arm. "They say I might need some physical therapy for my arm."

Rachel's eyes darkened with concern, warming Shane. "It must be very painful."

"It's okay. They're feeding me painkillers like candy. I don't feel a thing."

That wasn't exactly true. Because of his concussion he wasn't too heavily medicated. And Rachel either knew better or could see through his macho act because she looked twice as concerned now. She even seemed to have forgotten whoever was waiting for her down the hall. Looking into her blue eyes, Shane forgot everything, as well, thinking for the moment how he'd like to pull Rachel right down on the bed and show her just how good he actually felt.

*Squeak. Squeak.*

The sound of rubber-soled shoes coming to a halt in the doorway almost, but not quite, stole Shane's attention; had him silently cursing the arrival of the nurse. But it was the little voice calling that had the effect of a cold shower, making him jerk his head around to stare through the haze of resulting pain.

"Mommy."

*Mommy?*

"Rose." Rachel whirled from the bed and crossed the room. Shane's gaze riveted on the tiny figure standing in the doorway. The rubber-soled shoes he'd heard were pink sneakers, topped by frilly white socks. Blue eyes bright as stars returned his stare from beneath a thick fringe of gold bangs. Though dressed in ruffled denim, with chubby legs poking from beneath her skirt and a ponytail tied in pink ribbon at her crown, the little girl was a replica of Rachel. So much so, a person might wonder if anyone else at all had had a hand in her creation.

But of course, someone had. Watching Rachel lean down to murmur to her daughter, Shane understood now why there had been no barrage of questions about Laura. As an apparently single woman with a child, Rachel was probably accustomed to fielding questions herself. Shane knew he had a passel of them wanting to be asked right now.

A frazzled young nurse appeared in the doorway, looking down at Rose with exasperation. "I'm sorry. She was in the playroom with the games supervisor when she suddenly came running down the hall."

Rachel apologized while Shane grinned at the mental picture of the little girl being chased down the hall by the nurse. Rose was watching him and grinned, too.

"I can take her back if you're not finished with your visit," the nurse offered, her ruffled feathers soothed by Rachel's good manners.

"No, Mommy, I want to stay." Rose lifted her arms to her mother and Rachel gathered her up.

"I'll only be another minute," Rachel assured the young blond nurse, who hesitated, glancing for the first time at Shane. He gave her his best smile and the nurse stammered her permission, backing out of the room.

Rachel crossed the room slowly and Shane thought what a feminine picture she and Rose made in their blue dresses. But with the assessment came an instinctive warning stronger than the one elicited by Rachel's youth. Shane was the first to admit that, when Laura wasn't around, he enjoyed the company of women. But when it came to involvement of any kind, he was cautious about the partner he chose; and rule number one was he didn't choose women with children, all too aware that kids were easily hurt.

Rachel held Rose away, making Shane think similar thoughts might be going through her head. "Shane, this is my daughter, Rose. Rose, this is Shane, the cowboy who owns the brown horse in our barn."

Rose considered him from the safety of her mother's arms. Her gaze wavered between the bandage near his temple and the cast on his arm, finally settling with fascination on the cast. Shane smiled when Rose whispered, "Why does he have that, Mommy?"

"That's a cast to help Shane's arm get better." Rachel spoke softly and Shane noticed she was careful not to use the word *broken* when describing his arm. He figured she was ahead of the game, remembering how Laura had gone into hysterics once at about Rose's age when he'd shown his daughter the cast on his "broken" wrist, compliments of a bull at Amarillo.

"Does it hurt?" Rose continued in her stage whisper, peeking at him from the corner of her eye. Shane could tell Rose knew he heard her by the way her little lips pursed against a smile, but she pretended not to know, seeming to find the charade great fun.

"The doctor gave Shane medicine to make the hurt go away," Rachel answered patiently.

"I'm happy it doesn't hurt." Rose's whisper was very loud this time, making sure he heard her, and Shane's heart warmed.

Rachel put an end to the game, asking, "Is there anything we can get for you while we're here?"

Shane guessed she had noticed the absence of visitors, flowers, or the telephone ringing with well-wishers. He'd already called Laura where she and her mother lived at her grandparents' house in Guthrie. Not that his ex-wife, Lana, would care. There was really no other family except Laura to whom he mattered enough to call.

"Can't think of a thing, but thanks," Shane told Rachel. "The trooper brought my travel bag, and my truck and trailer have been towed to a garage. I'll be out of here by tomorrow and I'll get square with you then on the care of my horse."

Rachel looked dubious, and Shane wondered if it was because she doubted he'd pay her or doubted he'd get out of the hospital. He could have assured her he was as good as his word on both counts.

But his nurse chose that moment to walk in, with a small tray in her hands. A frown marred her forehead as she assessed the damage from his bath and noted the presence of a child in the room. With wordless censure, she strode to the foot of the bed. "It's time for your medication, Mr. Purcell."

There was a needle on the tray that Shane knew you could use on a horse and it hadn't passed Rose's notice; the little girl's expression was one of trepidation. Oddly, Rachel wore a similar look, and Shane wondered if she was one of those people who faint at the sight of a needle. He hoped she had the sense to put Rose down if she was and prayed he had the strength to leap out of bed to catch her if she did.

Fortunately, Rachel put a stop to that foolish notion, backing away from the bed. "We'll be going now. My place is about a mile toward Guthrie from where you had your accident. And my phone number is in the book. It's Rachel Callahan, but I guess the trooper told you that."

Shane bit back the temptation to make clear he'd found out her name at the rodeo. He thanked her again, vaguely aware that the nurse approached as Rachel was leaving the room, with Rose peeking sympathetically over her mother's shoulder. Shane gave Rose a wink, and was rewarded with a smile.

Shane sighed as they disappeared, for once letting the nurse do her job without giving her any trouble. He scarcely noticed when she left, his mind still on Rachel and Rose. That little girl was cuter than a new spring filly. And she was also the reason he needn't entertain thoughts about Rachel.

He had enough on his mind, anyway. The doctor predicted his arm would take a good two months to heal. Usually, he slowed down on his rodeoing in the summer, sticking close to Oklahoma once Laura was out of school; he could sometimes manage an extra weekend with her then, her mother permitting. But slowing down was a whole lot different than quitting for two months. Quitting left him little choice other than to return to his ranch in Nebraska, although how he was going to haul a horse with a torn shoulder clear to northwest Nebraska, driving a stick shift with one arm in a sling struck him as something of a challenge.

His head throbbing, Shane concentrated instead on the one bright ray in his life, his daughter Laura, and the two weeks that Laura would spend with him this summer. And he focused on his great hope for the future: that this visit would be the turning point that had Laura choosing to stay in the custody of her father.

## Chapter Two

The Callahan ranch sat on sunbaked rolling prairie; the hot rays seemed to fade the redwood color from Rachel's house even as Shane watched the place draw near.

He eased his foot off the accelerator of the rental car, aware of the dust kicking up from a lane that was more dirt than gravel. It wasn't that he cared about the car; he hated the minuscule black sedan that dented the crown of his favorite hat and yet, despite it's small size, made him feel like he was riding in a hearse. But he didn't want to send dust rolling into any house windows Rachel might have opened. His mother, God rest her soul, had taught him that much about women.

Shane braked to a stop when the drive dwindled away to a sporadic border of Indian blanket, the red-

and-yellow wildflower only emphasizing the washed-out appearance of the house. Beyond it, parked beneath a lone oak, was a mobile home like many ranches had for the hired help, although this one had a closed-up, unoccupied look about it. Across the way was a fenced pasture, the fifty-five-gallon steel barrels set up in a triangle there assuring Shane he'd found the right place. There was no sign of activity despite the two trucks parked near the barn: one, a new red Chevy; the other, an older model—white, and spotted with rust.

Shane unfolded his legs from the car, leaving his Stetson on the seat. He felt naked without it, but it rubbed the stitches on his bruised, aching head. He stood, feeling light-headed, and leaned against the car, thinking maybe he should have taken the doctor up on that invitation to stay another day at the hospital.

Voices—feminine voices—drifted from an old wooden barn that was nearly devoid of its coat of red paint, making it a perfect match for the house. The wide front doors were open and as Shane watched, Rose came running from the shadows of the barn into the noonday sun, skidding to a halt at the sight of him. She had on crisp coveralls and a pink T-shirt, her hair in what Shane decided must be her trademark ponytail, tied this time with fresh white ribbon. He grinned at her and she grinned back before obviously remembering there were precautions to observe and running back into the barn. Even as Shane pushed away from the car, he could hear her calling for her mother.

But it was a brunette, not Rachel, who walked out of the barn and Shane wondered at the disappointment that ran through him. Especially given the fact that the brunette was attractive, wearing black jeans that fit like a second skin and a yoke-fronted shirt that hugged full curves. With a flick of her head she tossed her long hair over her shoulder in that way cowgirls had of doing it without dislodging their hat. Shane felt a little annoyed with himself when the action didn't affect him any, didn't keep his gaze from straying to the barn door looking for Rachel.

The brunette favored him with a calculated smile that told Shane it didn't matter that he hadn't shaved this morning or tucked his faded red shirt into his jeans—a feat he hadn't had the patience for, one-handed. Then she called over her shoulder, "Rachel, your cowboy is waiting."

*Your cowboy.* Rachel wouldn't like that. For some reason, that fact had Shane grinning when he should have been irritated, also. The grin softened to a smile when Rachel appeared in the barn doorway, Rose riding her hip, their golden hair glistening brighter than the sun.

"Mr. Purcell. When I called the hospital to check on your condition, the nurse told me it would be another day before the doctor released you."

"It's Shane," he reminded her, unable to stop a spurt of pleasure over the fact that she'd bothered to check on him. "And I'd had my fill of the hospital."

Rachel nodded with understanding, leaving him to wonder if she might also have spent time there for some injury, although in his opinion childbirth had to be experience enough to warrant her empathy.

Rachel shot the brunette a look of veiled exasperation. "Shane, this is Wanda Baron. Wanda, Shane Purcell. You may have heard of Wanda. She's number three in the standings in barrel racing and her daddy ranches hereabouts."

Shane wasn't familiar with Wanda's place in the standings, but he'd heard her name bandied in back of the chutes when the boys got rowdy and loose-tongued. She was the kind that came under rule number two of women he didn't date. Shane gave a polite nod, thinking he recognized her now, from one rodeo or another.

Wanda said coyly, "I've seen Shane around. He starts every year out hot in Denver. Seen him out to the finals in Vegas a few years back." She gave Shane a smile that made him think she remembered a night he'd forgotten—except he knew better. Then she turned to Rachel. "I've got to hit the road. Sure you won't take over training that black gelding for me? Daddy insists the horse be taught to quit running by barrels, but I don't have time to work with him, competing the way I am."

Shane silently translated that to mean Wanda had ruined the black horse and was now competing on another. And she wanted Rachel to "fix" this one.

Shane decided "Daddy" must be tired of providing his daughter with new stock each time this happened.

"I'm real sorry, but, like I told you, Lilly broke her hip and I can't take on more boarders until I find someone to watch after Rose." Rachel's voice was firm, although Shane figured the words hadn't come easily, certain by the looks of the place that Rachel could have used the money she would have gotten for training the horse.

"Kids can be such problems, can't they?" Wanda sighed, as if she had a child of her own to judge by, although Shane was certain she didn't, his memory of her growing fresher all the time. Wanda played fast and loose with the cowboys, pretty much like his ex-wife, Lana, still did, Shane thought darkly, reminded of the poor example Lana set for Laura.

He had to bite back a grin, though, when Wanda absently patted Rose on the leg and the little girl's bottom lip thrust out in a pout, her small brows drawing into a frown. Oblivious to Rose's dislike, Wanda sauntered away. "See you around."

"You can check back with me in a week if you want," Rachel offered.

"I just might do that."

Shane shifted uncomfortably, feeling Wanda's gaze slide over him before she climbed into her truck—the new red one—wheeled it around and sped down the drive, leaving the three of them standing in a trail of dust. Rachel's sigh was audible. Shane figured she saw only dollar bills biting the dust.

As Rachel watched the red truck fade to a speck in the distance, Shane took the moment to appreciate the sight of her standing in the sun. There was a radiance in her delicate features, a set to her jaw that hinted of determination. With her hair brushed into a long loose braid that shimmered down her back, Rachel looked as feminine and sexy as any man could wish for, even in a plain white T-shirt and faded jeans worn over the tops of scuffed white boots.

Then he noticed Rose was tracking his every move, her gaze following the path of his, making him conscious of staring at Rachel. Rose looked at her mother, then her bright blue eyes locked with his, and in that moment Shane would have sworn the little girl knew exactly what he'd been thinking.

But that wasn't possible. Shane wiggled his brows teasingly at Rose just to prove it. It was worth the stab of pain at his temple when she giggled, hiding her face in her mother's shoulder.

Rachel seemed drawn back to the present by her daughter's antics. "I guess you'd like to see your horse," she said, her voice cool.

Shane figured Rose was the reason for her reserve. The sight of the little girl certainly had him drawing his loop back in.

Rachel led the way toward the barn. "The vet said to try and keep the horse quiet, but he seemed kind of restless so I put him in a foaling stall where he'd have more room to move around."

"Restless" didn't sound good, didn't sound like Cash, except at feeding time. Shane felt an apprehension reminiscent of when Laura had had her appendix taken out. He followed Rachel into the barn, which had a row of four stalls on each side, built of sturdy oak boards with bars on top that let the horses see out. Rachel stopped before one of the stalls. Shane drew a bracing breath and looked in at his horse.

Cash stood in the corner, his head hung low, but Shane saw quickly it was only because he'd pulled fresh hay from the bag hanging there. Still, the cut on Cash's shoulder was enough to have Shane releasing a soft whistle. The horse didn't look pretty with the yellow antibiotic powder dusted over his stitches, his brown hair shaved away from around the wound. Cash was homely at best, though, and Shane could see the vet had done a good job.

"Doc said the wound isn't all that deep."

A defensive note Shane recognized from the hospital crept into Rachel's voice again, and Shane wondered at how easily it was triggered.

"The horse will likely mend before I will," he assured her, making clear he found no fault with the care she'd given his horse. He tried not to think about the thousands of dollars the next two months were going to cost him.

Shane pulled a check from his shirt pocket and handed it over to Rachel. "Would you mind if I left Cash a few more days? It'll be that long before I get my truck repaired."

"There's more than enough here to cover a few days' board," Rachel told him after a glance at the check. Her drawl had softened, and Shane thought to himself that here was a woman whose voice he could listen to all day. "The vet seemed to think you'd be taking chances shipping the horse too soon, especially clear to—" she looked at the check again and gave a small smile "—the Purcell ranch in Nebraska."

Rose wiggled, wanting down, and Rachel obliged. Rose stood before the stall gate, calling Cash's name while the horse went on eating. Only half of the stalls were occupied, the tack hanging near each indicating the stage of training of the horse inside. Curious, Shane asked, "You train horses for a living?"

"Train, board, sell. Whatever it takes."

Which explained why her name wasn't a familiar one on the circuit. Out the window of the stall, the barrels set up in the pasture gleamed white with a stripe of red around the middle, the only things on the place sporting a decent coat of paint. Rachel's love for the sport was apparent and he suspected she would have found success as a barrel racer. She was struggling to get by, but Shane had to admire that she'd opted to provide a stable home for her daughter.

"My daddy set up barrels out there for me when I was five years old," Rachel said fondly, and Shane turned to find her gazing out the window, also. His mind cataloged the fact that she was living on her daddy's ranch, not that of some man she might have been married to. He wondered what circumstances had put Rose's father out of the picture, wondered if Rachel might be widowed, or divorced. But Rachel apparently misread the question in his eyes, explaining, "Daddy died just before Rose was born."

"He missed out on a lot," Shane observed gently, unable to keep from smiling at Rose's cooing attempts to coax Cash to the stall door. The little tyke obviously loved horses and it was easy to imagine Rose out there practicing the barrels someday, Rachel calling encouragement from her perch on the fence. Shane's gaze returned to the window. Considering his daughter's new passion for barrel racing, he knew Laura would love it here....

The thoughts and pictures in Shane's mind seemed to mesh as one, until he saw Laura riding the cloverleaf pattern under Rachel's instruction while he and Rose watched. The idea came over him then; a way that he could stay in Oklahoma, a way that Rachel could train her horses.

It was a crazy idea, of course. And Rachel would never agree.

"That mobile home of yours—I couldn't help noticing it was unoccupied," Shane said anyway. It wasn't the first time he'd gone with a crazy idea and most likely it wouldn't be the last.

"I sold some land a couple years ago. I haven't needed hired help since then." Rachel's tone stated clearly that she had no use for a hired hand now—especially one with a broken arm and a concussion.

Shane got the impression he wasn't the first cowboy to make Rachel a proposition.

"I was thinking," Shane said, trying another approach and choosing his words carefully, "that you probably would have liked to take over the training of that horse of Wanda's."

Rachel stared at him. But she didn't deny it, and Shane decided to take that as encouragement. "Most summers, I rodeo in Oklahoma to be near my daughter. Being busted up like I am has put a real kink in those plans. It seems coincidental, you having that trailer to rent and needing someone to watch over Rose, and me looking for a way to stay around Guthrie awhile."

Rachel's jaw went slack. Shane figured he'd taken her by surprise, but then, the idea had been somewhat of a surprise to him, also. Still, the more he thought about it, the more sense it made. "Laura stays with me for two weeks every summer. She's been showing a real interest in barrel racing. I think she might like spending those two weeks here."

Rachel's jaw snapped shut. She threaded her hand through her bangs and Shane wished he could read the thoughts running through her head. But she hadn't said no, and when her gaze slid to Rose, it seemed safe to assume Rachel was seriously considering the idea.

Shane said persuasively, "If I watch Rose, you could take that horse for pay. I'd be paying you rent, plus board for my horse, and maybe even some lesson money for working with Laura on the barrels."

"If you're so rich you can throw all that money around, you ought to be able to come up with something better than staying in that old trailer—not to mention baby-sitting," Rachel said, but her criticism lacked bite. She only needed a bit more convincing, Shane decided.

"Who says I'm rich? I was expecting a pretty big break on rent for keeping a watchful eye on your 'valuable,' there."

Rachel caught her lip and he knew she was tempted. "What makes you think I'd trust you with my child?"

This was the big one. "Because you've seen me with Laura and you can tell I'm a good father. And Rose likes me. We'd get along fine while you work the horses."

Rachel glanced at Rose; the little girl was slipping stray stems of hay to Cash, who had finally come to the stall door. Rose responded as if on cue, turning to smile at Shane. He could have kissed her.

"It wouldn't look right, you living here in that trailer," Rachel said firmly.

"You just said you had a hired hand living there a while back," Shane countered. "What's the difference?"

"That man was sixty years old, and he didn't—" Rachel faltered, and her gaze flickered over him.

*Didn't what?* Every inch of Shane's being responded to that hesitant awareness in Rachel's eyes. He swallowed hard and tamped down the desire that rushed over him.

"He didn't hire on as a baby-sitter," Rachel finished lamely.

He was wearing her down, Shane told himself. "I don't smoke and I won't drink. And the only company I'll be keeping is Laura's. You call any cowboy or cowgirl you know that's heard my name and they won't have anything bad to tell you. Just don't call my ex-wife," he added wryly.

That brought a reluctant smile to Rachel's lips. "I know all about exes." She sighed, then she raised her chin with new resolve. "But I can't agree to this. I don't even know if Rose would let you baby-sit her."

"Oh, hell, Rachel," Shane swore softly. "We'll play on the porch while you work the horses. Rose won't even know I'm watching her. And I swear, I'd keep her safe as if she were my own."

Rachel caught her lip. "I don't know...."

From the front of the barn, a telephone rang and Shane hoped the reprieve would have Rachel giving the idea more thought. She excused herself, admonishing Rose to stay put. Shane took it as a small sign of trust that Rachel had left Rose here, where he could watch over the little girl.

He listened to Rachel's murmuring voice, thinking of her soft sigh when she'd revealed that she, too, was divorced. His overall impression was that Rachel had it tough, and he liked knowing that his plan could help them both. He had no qualms about looking after Rose; he knew he could serve as a good male role model for the little girl. He just had to convince Rachel of that.

Thinking of the way Rose had of grinning at him, Shane smiled at her. He crouched beside the child, watching as Cash stole a hay stem from her grasp.

"Oh, hell," Rose swore softly.

## Chapter Three

Rachel hung up the telephone and looked down the length of the barn to see Shane hunkered down beside Rose like some big kid. They seemed deep in conversation and Rachel had to admit Shane was right. Rose did like him, and Rose wasn't usually that friendly toward men—a trait Rachel sometimes worried that she'd unconsciously instilled in her daughter.

Still, she must be crazy, giving thought to this idea of Shane's. Just because Rose liked him and just because she'd seen him laughing with his daughter didn't mean she should trust him to watch her child. She had to remember the other Shane, the one that rode bulls and charmed women. Rachel pursed her lips. Look how easily that blond-haired nurse at the hospital had fallen prey to his smile. Even Wanda remembered him, and Wanda knew every cowboy west of the Mississippi.

With that thought in mind, Rachel walked back to Shane, determined to turn him down.

"Mommy, look." Rose dipped her small hand into the pocket of Shane's red shirt, pulling out a cube of sugar. She laid it on her palm and held it under the stall gate for Cash. Rachel couldn't find fault with the way the horse carefully plucked the treat from Rose's hand. Rose beamed and asked Shane, "Can I give one to my kitty?"

"Kitties don't like sugar," Rachel said, and told herself it meant nothing that Shane carried sugar in his pocket for his horse. "You can give Princess some cat food while I talk to Shane."

Rose scampered off. Shane's dark head turned, following her path across the barn to the tin of cat food next to the grain bin. Rachel couldn't help noticing the way the strands of his black hair gleamed, couldn't help the tug of sympathy stirred by the bandage on his forehead and the sling he wore. His wide shoulders seemed to lift in a sigh, then he rose and faced her.

"Rachel..." Shane's voice slurred and his dark irises glazed over. He wavered and Rachel reached out her hand to steady him, her fingers closing over the firm round biceps of his good arm.

"Shane, you'd better sit down—"

He staggered and fell against her, his weight bearing her backward. Rachel caught him around the middle and their legs tangled in an awkward dance until the heavy press of Shane's body pinned her to the rough stall wall. Rachel shored him up with her arms, sweat beading on her brow from the effort.

He was heavy. And warm. His musky scent was thick on the air she dragged in, while his breath burned the side of her neck in hot quick puffs. She could feel the hard pressure of his cast across her chest, but it was the back of his hand resting against the swell of her breast that riveted her in place. His other arm was trapped at her back and her nose was nuzzled into his shirtfront as if he held her in an embrace. As if they were lying in bed . . .

Rachel raised her head, bumping Shane's chin. He transferred some of his weight to the wall, but his body still brushed hers from shoulder to knee, their boots nudged one against the other. His hand, splayed across her spine, felt hot.

"Sorry," Shane gasped, but Rachel figured the damage was already done. He was sprawled all over her and she felt on fire with his nearness.

"You have to sit down." Her heart was pounding and Rachel needed desperately for him to move away.

"Hold on. Don't want . . . to fall . . . and scare the kid." Shane's voice was thick, as if he struggled to regain his senses. Rachel swallowed, grateful for his concern for Rose and feeling foolish over the stirrings within her. Shane was likely in pain and obviously unaffected by their close proximity.

But when she looked into his eyes a moment later, there was no mistaking the awareness there. Shane's dark eyes gleamed. Mesmerized. Even as she felt the strength return to his body, he seemed to press closer, his knuckles settling more firmly against her breast, his other hand slipping farther down her spine. Rachel curled her fingers into the back of Shane's shirt, unclear in her foggy mind if she meant to pull him away or push him closer. There was a dusky shadow of beard on his upper lip and Rachel stared in fascination as his mouth made a slow descent toward hers, her eyes drifting closed with the feather-light brush of his lips upon hers.

Shane jerked away. Rachel's fingers slipped free of his shirt and a coolness rushed over her. She could feel hot color form on her cheeks and she lowered her gaze to the scarred toes of her boots.

"I never meant for that to happen, Rachel."

For some reason, Shane's apology struck a discord within her. Rachel glared up at him. "Oh, no? I don't think I've imagined the way you've looked at me."

"I won't deny I've been looking." Shane stared at her hard. "Any more than you can deny you were watching me at the rodeo."

Rachel's face grew hotter. She grasped at straws of pride, saying, "Then you realize why I have to turn down your offer. I have to consider what's best for Rose." Her glance fell upon her daughter, playing with the kitten, oblivious to the sparks and tension. Rachel wanted to preserve that innocence.

"If you'll recall, since meeting your daughter, I've been on my best behavior."

Rachel couldn't deny that was true. When Rose had appeared at the door of his hospital room, Shane had backed off like he'd hit a hot wire.

"What happened here was an accident," Shane went on, and his mouth curved wryly. "There isn't a man alive who could have resisted temptation just now."

His honesty was both flattering and humbling, but Rachel couldn't bring herself to make a similar admission. "I don't believe in asking for trouble," she told him instead. "It seems to come around on its own often enough."

"This is a chance to lighten the load, not add to it," Shane insisted. "You're forgetting, I've got Laura to think of. And you're wrong if you feel I wouldn't have the same regard for your daughter. The way I see it, we're two of a kind where our kids are concerned. We could help each other."

He sounded so reasonable, Rachel thought. Yet there was this voice inside her warning that Shane could hurt her, too, however unintentionally.

Shane sighed, apparently reading her reluctance. "I still need a place to keep my horse. Can I count on you for that?"

"Of course."

"Then I'll be heading back to town to see about my truck and trailer." Shane gave her a nod and turned away, his dizziness seeming to have abated. He called a goodbye to Rose, and Rachel watched with mixed reactions as her daughter came running to Shane's side.

"Where are you going?" Rose stood before him, her little hands clasped about nuggets of dry cat food.

"I'm going to Guthrie to check on my truck," Shane replied politely.

"Mommy said it ran into a tree."

"It sure did." Shane chuckled and Rachel couldn't help but respond to the smile he sent her. Then he returned his attention to Rose. "Tell you what. I'll leave my last piece of sugar with you if you'll feed it to Cash for me."

Rose nodded eagerly. "He likes me to feed him sugar."

Because Rose's hands were full, Shane took out the sugar cube and tucked it in a pocket of her coveralls. She favored him with a smile, then ran back to her kitten, leaving Rachel to think—despite her misgivings—that meeting Shane had been good for Rose.

Rachel walked with Shane to the barn door. He paused there and thanked her again for taking care of his horse. Then he said, "I hope you'll reconsider renting me that mobile home for a while."

Thinking of Shane's daughter, Rachel couldn't bring herself to say another outright "no." She skirted his question with one of her own: "What about your ranch in Nebraska? Surely you have responsibilities there."

"My main responsibility lives in Guthrie with her mother and grandparents," Shane said flatly.

He meant it, Rachel realized. He was determined not to let his injury send him miles away from his daughter this summer, to the point that he was willing to live in her run-down excuse of a trailer. She tried to imagine what it would be like, knowing he was living a hundred yards from her door, sleeping in that trailer's soft old double bed....

Shane sighed. "I've got a sizable acreage, but I've leased the land for grazing. I assume the house is still standing since the last tornado—in the spring I head down to Guthrie, around the time for the rodeo."

"I know," Rachel murmured, then blushed at the intent look he gave her. "I saw you at the rodeo in Guthrie. I was watching with friends. You were having a pretty good...*time*...night, if I remember right."

A shadow passed over Shane's face that denied the "good time." "Lana left town with Laura the week of the rodeo." Shane shrugged, but the pain in his voice belied the offhand gesture. "I usually skip Guthrie if Laura isn't around."

"I missed the rodeo a few years myself," Rachel grimly recalled, thinking how Jace hadn't wanted her associating with old friends who encouraged her interest in training horses. A little defiantly she claimed, "I had fun going this year. I took Rose to town for the parade."

"Guess I missed that part."

Rachel recalled the clinging women and the too-bright gleam in Shane's eyes the night of the rodeo. No, he hadn't been in the frame of mind for a parade.

But Rachel couldn't help thinking how she and Shane had missed seeing one another at Guthrie over the years, each caught up in the resulting webs of their divorces. The unexpected regret she was feeling seemed reflected in his eyes. Then he glanced away, saying, "Maybe I'll make it to the parade next year. Like I said, I only hang around Oklahoma for Laura's sake."

Shane walked to his rental car. With his hair falling over his bandaged forehead and his shirttail carelessly riding the seat of his jeans, he looked more dangerous than weak, but Rachel found herself calling after him, "Are you sure you feel okay to drive?"

Shane opened the car door and said meaningfully, "I'm fine now, Rachel. I just lost my head back there for a moment. I can promise it wouldn't happen again."

With that, Shane climbed in the car and Rachel watched him drive away. She believed his promise was sincere. She might be willing to take him up on his offer if she was certain she could promise the same.

Rachel returned to her chores. The day's work and play finally wound themselves down until she had Rose tucked into bed and had showered and taken her usual seat at the kitchen table. She seldom sat in the living room at night. The couch seemed long and empty when she curled up there alone. Rachel treasured the time when Rose sat long enough to be rocked and read a story before bed.

Tonight seemed especially lonely and Rachel knew it was because of Shane. A woman didn't have a man like Shane fall into her arms and kiss her, then walk away unaffected. But Rachel had succumbed to attraction before with Jace, only to find, too late, that she'd misjudged him. Now, growing up without a father, Rose was the one who suffered from her mistake.

Rachel sighed. In a couple of days, Shane would either find somewhere else to stay or haul his horse home. She was foolish to be sitting here, still thinking of his offer. But the thought kept running through her head that she could use the money Shane's presence would bring, especially if he watched Rose so she could get back to the business of training horses.

Rachel caught her lip. If she didn't start working those horses again soon, the few clients she had would be pulling out. She had to find a permanent sitter for Rose. Someone she could trust; someone Rose liked; someone like Shane . . .

Rachel's groan was drowned by the ringing of the telephone. She crossed the room to answer it, a tightness forming in her chest. No one called at this late hour except Jace, sometimes with the news that he wanted to spend a weekend with his daughter. Those calls had once been few and far between, but since Jace had remarried to an older, childless woman, the calls had come more frequently—a fact that made Rachel uneasy.

She lifted the receiver with trepidation. "Hello?"

"Rachel?"

The soft-spoken voice wasn't Jace's. Relief warmed her words as Rachel answered, "Shane. Where are you calling from?" She remembered how faint he'd been and easily envisioned him in the hospital again.

"My motel room."

Instantly, Rachel pictured a bare-chested Shane lounging against the pillows of the motel bed as he spoke.

"I thought I'd call and check on Cash."

Rachel blinked away her sexy vision of Shane before responding. "The horse is doing okay."

"That's good. I'm trying to swing a deal for a new pickup, an automatic. But the dealer has to contact my bank in Nebraska and do all the paperwork yet."

Rachel sighed enviously over the thought of a new pickup. Shane must have done well at the lucrative winter rodeos. But then, hadn't Wanda said he started every year out hot in Denver?

A muffled roar sounded in the background from over the phone. Rachel couldn't help wondering aloud, "Where are you staying?"

"A little place down the highway outside of Guthrie."

Rachel winced, guessing which place he meant. Obviously, he hadn't done well enough that he wanted to spend his money to stay somewhere nicer in town. He probably wouldn't get much sleep tonight between the traffic outside his window and the lumpy pillow beneath his already sore head.

Long seconds of silence passed and Rachel suspected Shane had guessed at her thoughts and was letting them play themselves out, hoping she'd give in and tell him he could rent her mobile home. Rachel shifted from one foot to the other, unable to decide what to do.

"You're awfully quiet," Shane finally said.

"I reckon you know why." Rachel sighed, her fingers tracing the faded flowers on her summer nightgown.

"I'm not pressuring you, Rachel. But I'm glad you're giving my idea some thought."

He sounded a little smug, like he knew she was going to cave in. Rachel crossed an arm below her breasts and cocked her head. "Tonight at supper Rose told me 'hell' was a bad word."

That took him down a peg, for Shane seemed suddenly stricken by a cough. Rachel pursed her lips to keep from smiling. She relented, telling him, "Rose also said you told her not to say it. She said you promised not to say it, either."

"I promised to try," Shane amended, and Rachel could hear the grin in his voice.

"She really likes you, Shane."

"I told you that."

"If you were to stay here awhile, you'd have to be careful with her feelings, especially when it came time for you to leave."

"I understand that. I wouldn't hurt Rose for anything."

Rachel believed him. "You can rent the trailer. We'll just have to see how it works out with Rose."

"Shoot, you may as well call that brunette and tell her to haul that horse over. Rose and I will get along fine."

"I'll have the trailer ready for you by tomorrow afternoon," Rachel answered noncommittally.

"I appreciate this chance to stay near my daughter," Shane said, the husky tones washing over Rachel like a warm summer rain. "And I meant what I said. I'd never hurt Rose. I don't plan to hurt *anyone.*"

They hung up after goodbyes. Rachel leaned against the wall, that old saying running through her head about even the best plans going astray.

# Chapter Four

Rachel paused in the sunny doorway of the barn and spanked the dust from her jeans. She peered from beneath her hat brim to the long shady porch where Shane sat in the swing watching Rose play with a doll. Or rather, playing with Rose and the doll. His big hand swallowed up the doll's middle as he held it while Rose brushed its bright yellow hair. Her daughter's laugh drifted to her and a mix of feelings came over Rachel; that worn regret for what might have been, a sense of hope for what could be....

She needed a break, Rachel thought, blaming her errant thoughts on the heat. She looked in on the horse she'd just ridden, then tossed her hat on a hay bale and headed for the house. Rose and Shane had disappeared inside. Rachel gave a wry smile. If she listened closely, she knew she'd hear the lid on the cookie jar rattle.

Rachel let herself in quietly and went to lean in the kitchen doorway. With the doll tucked under his arm, Shane handed a cookie down to Rose, his dark hair falling over his forehead. It had been only four days since he'd arrived and he still wore that rakish bandage over his stitches. And he wore his shirts with the pearl snaps neatly fastened, but hanging loose from his jeans so she was always catching glimpses of flat belly and taut hips beneath the shirttails. She'd found it to be a real torment, watching those shirttails flap.

Rose reached for her cookie and Rachel said, "You're spoiling my daughter."

Shane straightened, the proverbial boy caught with a hand in the cookie jar. But it wasn't the look of a boy she saw when his eyes gleamed at her a moment later. Rose snatched the cookie from his hand and darted from the room, leaving Rachel alone with Shane, listening to the sound of cartoons coming on in the living room and the sudden pounding of her heart.

"These are oatmeal cookies." Shane set aside the doll and got another cookie. He stepped close and held it out to Rachel. "You told me Rose had oatmeal for breakfast. Can't be much difference."

The glint in his eyes was teasing, not flirtatious, Rachel told herself. But her body wasn't responding appropriately; her skin was warming, her mouth going dry. Rachel licked her lips and took the cookie.

"I've been meaning to tell you—you don't have to be graining the horses in the morning for me before you watch Rose. You probably shouldn't be doing that anyway, considering your injuries."

Shane shrugged that notion aside. "It works out fine—you and Rose have breakfast together, Rose and I share cookies. You make good cookies, Rachel."

"Thanks." Rachel pushed her damp bangs from her forehead, felt her braid lying hot against her back through the cotton of her sleeveless white shirt. The house felt unusually warm despite the breeze flowing through the screened windows.

"We made lemonade, too." There was an icy pitcherful on the counter, next to a spoon and her sugar bowl. Shane turned to open a cupboard, taking down glasses one at a time with his good hand. Four days, and he already knew where everything was in her kitchen. Rachel sipped the lemonade Shane gave her and watched him drain a glassful, the muscles of his throat working when he swallowed, his lips glossy when he set the glass aside.

"It's too sweet," Rachel informed him. But she kept sipping.

"I like it that way."

Those dark eyes of his were sparkling again. A girl might almost think he referred to something other than lemonade. Rachel finished her drink, keeping to herself the fact that she liked it—lemonade—that way, as well. "Make sure Rose brushes her teeth."

Rachel set her glass near the stove, not about to reach past Shane to put it on the counter. She went into the living room to kiss and hug Rose, then headed for the door. When Shane met her there, Rachel told him, "Wanda's coming to see her horse ridden. After that I'll be able to take care of Rose."

"No hurry."

But Shane frowned and Rachel waited, expecting some problem concerning Rose.

Instead Shane warned her, "Be careful with that black gelding. I've noticed he's damn skittish."

Rachel pressed a finger to her lips and glanced toward the living room.

"*Darn* skittish. Don't trust him, Rachel."

Shane's concern sent a new wave of warmth coursing through Rachel; a more mellow warmth, but one she found no less disturbing. Forcing a coolness to her voice, Rachel assured him, "I can handle the horse."

"If you want some help with him—"

"I can handle everything on my own."

Rachel pushed her way out the door, repeating the words to herself as she crossed to the barn, aware Shane watched her until she disappeared inside.

Wanda didn't show up until Rachel was cooling out the black gelding, walking him along the sand perimeter of the pasture that served as her arena. The sun was getting high in the sky and Rachel was hot and ready for lunch and a little irked that Wanda was more interested in talking to Shane than discussing the progress of the horse. Shane had wandered down earlier with Rose, but now Rose was playing by the barn door with her kitten and Shane and Wanda were cozied up to the fence like two doves roosting.

Wanda laughed and leaned lightly against Shane's injured arm. Shane's gaze was hidden and Rachel seethed, wondering if his eyes shone at Wanda the way they'd seemed to at her in her kitchen. She wasn't going to put up with any shenanigans on her ranch when she had an impressionable daughter to think of.

"Rosebud!"

Shane stepped away from the fence as he called and Rachel watched Rose come running with her kitten, her little red cowgirl boots churning up dust, her ponytail bouncing beneath the denim bow that matched her jeans. Shane scooped her up, kitten and all, and turned back to the fence with Rose now positioned between him and Wanda.

Almost as if, Rachel thought with a quick beat of her heart, he was using Rose as a buffer between him and Wanda. Rachel studied her daughter's frowning face. Funny, she'd never noticed before, but Rose didn't seem to like Wanda....

Rachel dismounted and led the horse through the gate. Shane walked over, with Wanda stuck to his side like a burr, and said, "Rose is hungry. I can strip down the horse if you want to take her inside while you and Wanda talk."

Wanda snatched the reins from Rachel's hand and smiled like the cat who'd found the cream. "I'll stay and help with my horse."

Once again, impatience swept over Rachel and, although she didn't like giving in to the feeling, it seemed to consume her, to prod her to say, "I'd appreciate a hand, Wanda. Shane, you can take Rose on up to the house—that is, if you don't mind." *If you're sure you wouldn't rather stay with Wanda.*

Shane grinned at her and the smugness she saw there made Rachel want to slap his handsome face. She all but snapped at him, "You can hardly take care of the horse with your arm in a sling."

"Oh, you'd be surprised what I can do with my arm in a sling," Shane drawled, and he sauntered away, letting Rose deposit her kitten at the barn door before carrying the child to the house. Rose waved over his shoulder and Rachel unclenched her hand to wave back.

Wanda pouted and didn't stay long, much to Rachel's relief. She finished her noon chores and went to the house, surprised by the quiet that greeted her there. There were no sounds coming from the kitchen and Rachel hung her hat on a wall hook and peeked into the living room.

Shane and Rose were asleep, her daughter tucked next to him on the couch, his good arm curved protectively over her. Rose's tiny boots lay next to his on the floor and her stocking feet rested upon his thigh. Shane's chin just brushed the top of Rose's head and his jaw was lean and shadowy next to her soft, fair hair, as his breath lightly stirred her silky bangs.

Rachel crossed the room and knelt on the hardwood floor beside them. She wasn't surprised to find Rose sleeping deeply, but she worried over how soundly Shane slept, the white bandage on his forehead half hidden by the dark strands of his hair. He still had to be suffering from the effects of his concussion.

But Shane looked amazingly content despite the fact that he was cramped against the back of the couch and sleeping in his jeans. Rachel hated falling asleep in her jeans—a person might as well sleep in starched pajamas. But Shane didn't appear uncomfortable at all. His jeans looked soft; the faded denim clung smoothly to his firm contours. Where his shirttails parted, the waistband of his jeans gapped slightly away from his bare, flat belly....

Shane suddenly raised his hand and Rachel started at the touch of his fingers sliding along the side of her neck to thread in her hair.

"Shh." Shane glanced down at Rose and whispered, "Don't wake her. I'll get up in a moment."

Rachel relaxed, giving in to the gentle pressure he exerted.

"Rose was tired after she ate. I didn't mean to fall asleep, but she wanted me to lay down by her."

"That's what I usually do," Rachel assured him, her voice hushed. "Did she eat a good lunch?"

"We both did." Shane grinned. "I hope you don't mind."

"I don't mind."

Shane shifted a little and their faces were suddenly close enough she could see a spark shining through the sleepy haze in his eyes.

Rachel swallowed hard. She was coming to know that look in his eyes. She'd seen it that very first day in her barn, when he'd fallen into her arms. When he'd kissed her...

But he couldn't be going to kiss her now. She smelled like sweat and sunscreen and horses. She probably had chaff in her hair. Yet she felt the press of each of his fingers through her hair, the warmth of his palm burning her neck. She wondered how Rose didn't wake from the crackle of tension between them. "Shane—"

He tugged her close and his mouth settled over her lips, still pursed in the whisper of his name. Rachel sagged against the couch, aware of Rose sleeping just inches below the canopy they formed with their kiss, aware of the birds chirping outside the open windows, aware that beyond those windows daylight burned as bright and hot as the flame leaping inside her. This was no time of day—no time in her life—to be kissing a man like Shane Purcell, a man she didn't really know....

Rachel caught Shane's hand and drew it away, leaning back and staggering to her feet. Shane dropped his arm over his eyes and she watched his chest lift and fall on a heavy breath. He untangled himself from beside Rose, who curled up and reached in her sleep for the doll Shane picked up off the floor and held out to her. He tucked it beside Rose and Rachel couldn't help thinking how naturally he cared for her daughter.

His kisses came naturally, too. Rachel hugged her arms across her middle. Keeping her voice low, she reminded him, "You said you wouldn't let that happen again."

Shane pushed a hand through his tousled hair. "I didn't mean to. You were just so...close. I could smell your hair—"

"I smell like a horse."

He smiled. "Sunshine. You smell like sunshine, Rachel."

"Shane—"

"Look, this was an accident, like before. You caught me by surprise."

"You caught hold of me, if I remember right."

He ignored that and said, "We just have to keep out of reach a little better."

Rachel eyed Shane skeptically. He made it sound simple. But other than Shane's kiss, the past four days *had* gone smoothly. Rose was happy and that mattered more than anything to Rachel. "I guess you're right."

"I am. This means a lot to me, being here near Laura. Her mother's agreed to let her spend a weekend here soon. I won't do anything—anything more—to jeopardize that."

Shane gathered his boots and went outside to sit on the porch step, one-handedly pulling the broken in leather over his socks while Rachel watched through the screen. He rose and without a backward glance, headed for the trailer.

Rachel wondered if she would see Shane again that day. But later when she walked with Rose to the barn to do evening chores, Shane was already there. He appeared in the doorway of the barn and looked up at the sky, to the dark clouds rolling in on a gust of westerly breeze that lifted his black hair in a dance across his forehead.

Rose ran to Shane, stepping on his boots as she hugged his leg. "Can I have sugar for Cash?"

"In my pocket, Rosebud." Shane knelt and let her fish out sugar cubes. "Remember to hold your hand flat with your fingers down."

"So he can't bite me," Rose quoted. But she didn't seem very worried over the prospect as she trotted into the barn, the sugar cubes cupped in her hands.

*Rosebud*. Rachel sighed. She'd heard Shane call Rose that twice now. It was a sweet nickname, something a father might call a daughter, something Jace had never grown close enough with Rose to do. Jace had always made threats to take Rose, but Rachel had often wondered if he really realized what he was missing.

"Rain's coming." Shane was looking at the sky again, those damn shirttails whipping with the breeze.

Rachel lifted her face to catch the coolness, but it didn't quite reach to the heat that lingered inside her. "We need a good rain."

"They're calling for thunderstorms on the radio. I'll finish up here and you can get Rose back to the house."

Even as he spoke, there was a rumbling in the sky. Inside the barn, Rachel could see Rose raise her head in apprehension and the instinct to carry her off to the house was strong. Still, Rachel hesitated; another instinct, one of self-preservation, kicked in. "There's no need for you to do my chores."

Shane regarded her quietly and Rachel sensed he could read every thought that rushed through her mind. Then, with an unexpected stubbornness, he told her, "I'm going to give you a hand to beat this rain."

And there was no arguing, for Shane walked off into the barn. Rachel stared after him, uncertain whether to insist or to follow. Lightning flickered from the clouds and thunder rolled. Rachel flinched, ducking into the barn.

Shane was measuring out grain and dumping it into the feed mangers. There seemed nothing awkward about his movements despite the fact that he went about the task one-handedly. His sureness added to his determined air. Rachel got busy filling water buckets with the hose, silently fretting over Shane's help, assuring herself she could handle the situation if he wasn't here. Another crackle and boom from outside brought Rose running to her side.

Shane grasped the hose from Rachel's hand. "Take Rose on up to the house before this storm cuts loose."

Rachel gathered up her daughter. Rose wound her arms tightly around her mother's neck and cut off any lingering protests. "All right."

Rose had a protest of her own. "I want to bring my kitty!"

Shane ruffled her bangs. "I'll take care of Princess. I'll make sure she's safe in her box." He glanced outside where drops of rain were starting to fall. "You girls go on, now."

Rachel hesitated, suddenly realizing Shane's bandage would get wet, that he'd be struggling to close the big barn doors against the wind with one arm in a sling. Thunder rolled ominously. Rose cowered into her shoulder and Shane repeated, "Go on, Rachel."

She went. And it seemed a long way to the house with the sky low and alive with turbulence. Rachel dashed up the porch steps just as the rain fell in sheets.

Inside, she tended to Rose, then went to watch out the kitchen window for Shane. When he appeared Rachel caught her lip, gripping the sill while he swung the heavy barn doors shut, the rain soaking his hair and clothes. He ran for the trailer and she struggled to see between flashes of lightning, the rain all but obliterating the security light near the barn. Shane was slipping and sliding in the mud. When he disappeared around the corner of the trailer Rachel pressed her cheek to the window. The trailer lights came on and Rachel leaned back and let out a pent-up breath.

Shane had gotten the phone hooked up in the trailer so that he could keep in touch with Laura. Maybe she should call him and make sure he was all right. Rachel went to the phone, then hesitated. Shane would want to get dry, maybe take a warm shower....

The phone shrilled and Rachel jumped. She snatched the receiver off the hook. "Yes?"

"It's Shane."

"Shane." Rachel silently chastised herself for sounding so worried. "I saw your light come on." Now she sounded too relieved. "Did you find the matches and candles in case the electricity goes out?" *Mother hen,* Rachel groaned to herself.

"I'm all set. I'm just getting out of these wet clothes."

*Right now?* Rachel envisioned him pulling off his shirt as they spoke, the phone cradled between his neck and damp bare shoulder. His jeans would be next....

"Are you and Rose all right?"

Rachel closed her eyes briefly. "Yes, we're fine."

"Call if you need me. If not, I'll see you in the morning, Rachel."

It had been a long time since there had been someone to call on a stormy night if need be. After supper, Rachel read stories to Rose in the rocking chair until her daughter drifted to sleep. She carried Rose to bed and made her way to her own.

Pulling the sheet up to her chin, Rachel lay awake and recalled the big house in Guthrie where she'd lived with Jace until just before Rose was born. She'd missed this ranch, but since she'd left Jace and returned here soon after her father died, the isolation had worried her, especially with her father's ranch hand gone. Now she listened to the storm whip past the corners of the house and couldn't help but appreciate the presence of a man—even an injured one who spoiled her daughter.

Rachel frowned, thinking of the way Rose had taken to Shane. She was going to have to remind him that she didn't want Rose hurt over his leaving. The events of the day replayed themselves through her mind and Rachel knew she was going to have to work harder not to depend on Shane, to "keep out of reach." She didn't want to be hurt over his leaving, either.

Still Rachel lay a long time, thoughts of Shane, of his kiss, keeping the storm at bay.

## Chapter Five

Shane brushed a strand of Rose's gold hair from her cheek as she drifted to sleep on the quilt he'd spread over the porch for her and her dolls. He'd missed out on a lot of this caretaking with Laura when Lana had been granted custody. He couldn't help but enjoy filling the void with this little Rosebud.

Settling back in the swing, Shane rested a booted foot across one knee and regarded Rose with a grin. She looked like a ladybug in her red romper with its black polka dots. As always, there was a matching bow in her hair.

His gaze drifted toward the pasture, to the shine of Rachel's hair. Caught in a silver barrette below her straw hat, it had a fourteen-karat glitter in the sun as it streamed down the back of her pale denim shirt.

Rachel sat astride the black gelding as he pranced in place at the gate where she'd positioned him for a run at the barrels. Rachel shoved down her hat and with an imperceptible cue, sent the horse racing toward the first barrel, setting him on his haunches in a sliding stop as he neared that point where he would have run on by it. There they stood, Rachel patting the gelding's glossy neck before she walked him around the barrel and lit out for the next, repeating the stop-and-go process until she'd completed the cloverleaf pattern.

Afterward, Shane could see the horse prick its ears in interest. In the week since Wanda's visit, Rachel had the horse looking to turn those barrels again.

She praised the gelding for a moment, then guided him along the fence line in a walk. Right now, he plodded like a plow horse and Shane would have sworn Rachel was about to fall asleep in the saddle. But that spoiled gelding of Wanda's had a tendency to shy over nothing and Shane frowned, wishing Rachel wouldn't give the horse so loose a rein—

Brown fur flashed beneath the horse's hooves and the gelding whirled. Shane whipped out of the swing, remembered Rose and stilled. He whispered a curse and his gaze seesawed between Rachel and Rose. Rachel rode out the spin, then the horse got his head down for an almighty buck that sent her somersaulting to the ground. With a glance at the sleeping Rose, Shane leaped from the porch and sprinted toward the pasture.

Shane rushed through the pasture gate. Rachel rose to a sitting position and his erratic heartbeat slowed to a pound that made his temples throb. The gelding crow-hopped to the other side of the pasture and lowered its head to graze along the grassy fence border. Rachel cursed the horse soundly.

Normally, Shane would have laughed over that pretty drawl cursing the horse's pedigree. Now he looked down at Rachel, her nose powdered with Oklahoma dust, and all he could think was how that small nose could have been broken, along with several other bones in her featherweight body. Her hat was ten feet away, its crown tramped in. She was damn lucky her head wasn't still under it.

Like an aftershock, reaction set Shane's emotions rocking from relief to fear and back again until the throb in his temples spread to encompass his whole head. The cumulative effect was anger. Shane reached down and grasped her arm and hauled Rachel to her feet. "What the hell did you think you were doing?"

For a moment, he seemed to have taken her by surprise. Then Rachel jerked free and said hotly, "I was trying to teach that horse some manners."

"You were trying to get yourself killed, loose-reining him like he was some kind of pet-show horse!"

"I know the difference between—"

"You don't just throw the reins away—"

"Don't tell *me* how to train a horse—"

"You've got no business—"

"And don't *ever* tell me what to do!"

They were shouting, sweating, crowding each other, and now a sudden silence reigned. Shane towered over Rachel, holding her gaze, and he realized with blinding insight that she was looking at him with more anger than the situation warranted.

Abruptly, Rachel backed away, but not before Shane saw hurt and confusion cloud her eyes. She pushed her bangs from her damp forehead and her gaze focused sharply. "Where's Rose?"

*Good Lord.* He'd forgotten about Rose. Shane tossed a panicky glance over his shoulder. She was still sleeping on the blanket. Shane stiffened his momentarily weak knees and told Rachel grimly, "It was a hell of a choice to make, but I had to leave her sleeping on the porch to go see if her mama got kicked in the head."

"As you can see, I'm fine." Rachel pushed past him and limped over to snatch up her hat, punching out the crown. Shane held his tongue over her halting steps when she crossed to the horse, damned if he'd give her reason to snap at him again. But it was all he could do to just stand and watch when she caught the gelding and swung back into the saddle. She rode over and once she stopped, the horse stood at attention, as if aware he'd already caused enough trouble.

"Rose is the one who needs a baby-sitter," Rachel said pointedly and Shane's temper flared. As he glared at her, wisps of hair fluttered against Rachel's cheek. A trickle of sweat trailed down to her throat and disappeared into the shadowy vee of her shirtfront. The sight mixed with his rolling emotions had Shane fighting the sudden urge to yank Rachel from the saddle and into his arms, to cover her sassy mouth with his.

"I'll take care of Rose," Shane growled. "Just watch yourself with that horse."

He strode away, feeling sweat gather beneath the neck of his red shirt. His skin itched inside the cast, but Shane knew it wasn't the only itch he had that he couldn't scratch. He still wanted Rachel. Staying here was a big mistake.

But it was hard to hold on to that thought when he considered Laura and when he sank to the porch step near Rose, still sleeping beside her doll.

Shane ran his hand through his hair. He stared across the yard to the pasture, watching Rachel cool out the gelding, and he thought how she'd looked at him—through him—when they'd argued, her eyes full of old hurt. What had she said about training the horse? *Don't tell me what to do.* It didn't take a psychologist to figure out that she'd had problems with her ex-husband over how she ran her life.

Rachel had spoken only sparingly of Jace Callahan, revealing that they'd met at a ranchers' barbecue and divorced before Rose was born. Shane suspected the wealthy oilman was the driving force behind her every emotion. He didn't like the idea that her feelings about Jace colored the way she felt toward *him*.

Rose stirred and it appeared her short nap was over when she opened her eyes wide. "I want Mommy."

Shane looked back at Rachel and caught her glancing away. She dismounted from the horse and even in dusty, faded jeans her curves burned like a brand in his mind, had his blood heating. "How about we go get the mail for your mama first, Rosebud?"

Rose smiled, and Shane knew she liked both their daily trip down the lane and the nickname that had come naturally to him. She was a little flower waiting to bloom into full beauty, like her mother. Realizing Rose was already headed down the steps, Shane hastened to follow, having learned Rose could disappear faster than a burst bubble when a guy wasn't watching. He walked behind her, careful to shade her from the sun. She had Rachel's fair skin.

Shane shoved his good hand in his front jeans pocket. He was spending too much time thinking about the way Rachel looked, the way she talked, the fresh way she smelled early in the morning when he came to watch Rose. It was damn hard to keep away from a woman who affected his every sense.

They'd reached the mailbox and Rose lifted her arms, waiting. Shane hoisted her up to open the box. There was one white envelope and Rose pretended to read, then announced, "It's for Mommy."

Shane read the return address. The letter had come from Guthrie, from Jace Callahan. Sunlight shone through the envelope and Shane thought he could make out a check. Judging by the looks of Rachel's place and the stack of bills she kept next to her sugar bowl, he'd bet it wasn't alimony.

Rose wanted to get down to find shiny rocks and Shane obliged her, pondering over the check in his hand as they walked. He surveyed Rose's crisply ruffled romper. He'd never seen Rose dressed in anything but the best, while Rachel's clothes often had a well-worn look about them. It wasn't hard to imagine Rachel refusing anything but child support from the man who had put that hurt look in her eyes.

Ahead, Shane heard the screen door bang. He herded Rose toward the house and up the porch steps and after a quick knock, followed the little girl inside. Rose ran to turn on her cartoon and Shane went to the kitchen where he found Rachel talking on the telephone. He listened to her stubborn wheeling and dealing over a ton of grain and wondered if she was still mad at him.

A moment later she hung up the phone. Favoring her right leg, she turned to open a cupboard, rattling the pans inside. She was still mad. Shane leaned in the doorway. Figuring he had nothing to lose, he commented, "I notice you're still limping."

"It's an old knee injury," Rachel said curtly.

Shane rubbed his thumb over Jace's check and suspected it wasn't the only old hurt Rachel harbored. "I couldn't help overhearing you on the phone just now. You ought to get together with some other small ranchers to buy grain in bulk. You'd have more bargaining power."

Rachel had filled a pan half full of hot water and now she plunked it on the stove. "I prefer not to."

The chill in her voice somehow heated his temper. "Independent to a fault, aren't you, Rachel?"

Rachel measured out macaroni and dumped it into the pan. "I've found independence to be an advantage, not a fault."

Shane released an impatient breath and pushed away from the door. "I still think you ought to—"

"Stop it." Rachel faced him, her hand raised in a staying gesture. "Stop telling me what to do."

Shane understood where her stubbornness came from and he sympathized with her frustration. But he wasn't immune to the sharp stab of her words. Slapping Jace's letter onto the kitchen table he warned, "I was only trying to help. Don't go judging me by another man's actions."

Shane left her staring at the letter and strode out of the house. He went to the trailer and showered for a trip to the doctor. Minutes later, he wheeled his new black Chevy pickup down the drive, heedless of the spraying gravel.

Shane gripped the steering wheel. The miles sped by. Thoughts of Rachel filled his mind. Maintaining a physical distance from her was trying enough. But he hadn't counted on the emotional pull he felt whether Rachel was near or far. He could feel it clear across the pasture when she worked; could feel it now as if she were only a heartbeat away.

Shane's anger faded to a regret that had him wanting to turn the truck around. He reminded himself that his stay at the ranch was temporary. Rachel was right, anyway. Since her divorce she'd proved that she could handle things on her own.

By the time his stitches were removed Shane had come to the conclusion that a truce of sorts was necessary if he didn't want to lose this chance to be near Laura. It was almost suppertime. He picked up a bucket of fried chicken and some of Rose's favorite vanilla pudding and headed back to the ranch.

Rachel was sitting on the porch swing when he returned. Shane parked the truck at the edge of the yard. Rachel was wearing a fresh pink shirt and jeans and her hair spilled over one shoulder, free of its braid. Before he could stop himself, Shane thought how it would feel to run his hand down the length of silken strands. Then he noticed Rachel's bowed head and her hands clenched in the lap of her jeans.

Shane climbed from the truck, his anticipation replaced by trepidation as he scanned the porch for Rose. Rachel loved to sit on the porch in the evening while Rose played. But Rose was nowhere in sight.

Shane gathered the food in the crook of his arm and strode to the long low porch, taking the stairs and crossing to Rachel. The evidence of tears on her cheeks stopped him in his tracks. His first panicked thought was that something had happened to Rose.

Shane abandoned the food on the porch rail and knelt before Rachel. He gripped her arm. "Where's Rose?"

Rachel drew a shuddery breath, the sound reaching straight to his heart. Shane steeled himself and gave her a little shake, his unease escalating. "Has something happened to Rose?"

"No. No." Rachel caught her lip in an obvious struggle to hold herself together. "Jace came. He took Rose for the weekend."

Shane closed his eyes briefly. Rose was all right. Rachel was just missing her daughter terribly—a feeling he could too easily relate to.

Fresh tears rolled down Rachel's cheeks and Shane felt suddenly as useless as a lame horse. He recalled one of the few times his mother had cried, how his father had consoled her with a gentle touch. He tried to do the same now, easing his grip on Rachel's arm, soothing her with the stroke of his thumb on her skin. She tried to be so tough. But she was all woman, softhearted, her skin smooth beneath his hand....

"I know Rose is fine." Rachel swiped at a tear, drawing another of those heart-wrenching breaths. "It's just . . . I'm afraid."

Her last whispered words had Shane leaning close, frowning a little. There were a lot of things a single parent could be scared over. "Afraid of what?"

"That Jace will take custody of Rose from me."

"Rachel, he can't just take Rose out of your custody."

"He's threatened to many times." She looked up at him, her gaze full of her fears. "Jace remarried recently. And Rose just adores his wife, Elizabeth."

The thought of Jace making threats to take Rose had Shane surging to his feet. He pushed a hand through his hair and told himself to go easy. Careful of Rachel's sore knee, he sat on the swing and faced her, one leg folded up on the seat, his good arm braced across the back. "Judging by my own experience, the mother often gets custody of the child."

Rachel glanced up at him in question and Shane had the unaccustomed urge to tell *his* story. Instead he went on, "You're a *good* mother. No court is going to take Rose from you. Jace has no grounds to take her."

Rachel dropped her gaze and a sense of misgiving came over Shane. But he couldn't imagine anything Rachel might have done that would jeopardize her custody of Rose. It just wasn't in her to do anything immoral or illegal. Still, for some reason, she was afraid. Shane laid his hand upon her shoulder. "Do you want to tell me about it?"

For a moment, he thought she might shut him out, and Shane was struck by how much he wanted Rachel to confide in him; how much he'd come to care about her and Rose.

Rachel looked out over the pasture. "I was working a horse one day. He was real green, just a three-year-old, and a little silly like that horse of Wanda's. Something set him off and he climbed right over that fence with me in the saddle. He broke down the fence and fell on the other side, on my knee."

Shane winced, having seen some knee injuries among rodeo cowboys, understanding now how Rachel had come by her "old injury."

"Rose was just a baby then," Rachel went on. "When I got out of the hospital I couldn't work, couldn't afford to have Lilly watch her. And it was hard to watch her myself, the pain was so bad, the therapy so difficult. I was scared Jace would find out. I had medication. I found if I took enough, I could take care of my baby...."

Rachel looked so ashamed it wasn't hard to see what had happened. She'd become addicted to the painkillers so that she could take care of Rose. No wonder she'd been sympathetic over his injuries that day at the hospital. Shane ached for her, hated to think how hard times had been for Rachel.

"When I went to the hospital for help with my addiction, Jace found out. And it's been his ace in the hole ever since."

Anger rippled through Shane. "You got over the addiction, Rachel. You've made a good home for Rose."

"Not as good a home as Jace Callahan can provide."

Her bitterness triggered his own. "Money talks."

Rachel looked at him then and Shane sighed. "I don't mean to scare you. But I understand your concern. The Blackwells, my ex-wife's parents, are very wealthy. They helped Lana gain custody of Laura.''

Rachel leaned her head against the back of the swing and Shane felt the brush of her hair on his hand. Softly she asked, ''What happened?''

It seemed natural now to tell her. ''Lana ran off with some cowboy when Laura was still a baby. She took Laura when she left.''

''What did you do?''

''I eventually found Laura and Lana at the Blackwells' house in Guthrie. They wouldn't let me see Laura or talk to Lana. I lost my temper and dented up Lana's sports car with a horseshoeing rasp.''

Shane grimaced, remembering. Aware Rachel stared at him, he explained, ''I don't usually have a short temper, except where Laura is concerned.''

''I know,'' Rachel replied. ''I'm having trouble picturing you smashing up that car.''

''It's not hard for me to recall. It took me two years to pay for the repairs.''

Rachel chuckled then and Shane smiled. He didn't usually talk about his family situation. But he'd never known a woman who would really understand. Rachel understood. ''Anyway, despite all of Lana's affairs and the fact that she wasn't much of a mother to Laura, her parents were able to help her gain custody.''

Shadows darkened Shane's gaze and Rachel could see the toll Shane's divorce had taken. The past had etched itself on his handsome face.

Rachel noticed then that Shane's bandage was gone; only a thin scar showed beneath the hair that fell over his forehead. She could tell where the bandage had protected his skin from the sun, could see how his brows were as black as his hair, his lashes thick and dark....

Shane's long lashes blinked and Rachel drew a quick breath, dropping her gaze from his. She realized that she was leaning very close to Shane's shoulder, that his hand was stroking her hair. For once he'd tucked in his shirt, and the sight of the crisp white cotton belted into the slim waist of his jeans was enticing enough to rivet her gaze on his trophy buckle. Heat gathered where his knee pressed her thigh, and the thought moved slowly through her mind that she ought to move away....

"Rachel?"

Shane's voice was gentle, but Rachel straightened, startled. Her mind raced in her flustered attempt to recall their conversation. "Laura—you mentioned once that she lives with her grandparents in Guthrie?"

"Her mother lives there, too, when she's not off with some new man. Gus and Emma care for Laura most often. They've got a big house with a swimming pool. I don't worry that Laura wants for anything."

Rachel saw through his words with a clarity born of her own fears. "You worry that she doesn't want you. That they've won her away with all they have to offer...."

"That's not going to happen with Rose," Shane insisted, clearly reading her fears.

"And I'm sure it hasn't happened with Laura."

"I'm hoping this summer she'll decide to stay with me. She's looking forward to coming here. I've told her you train horses and about those barrels set up in your pasture. I'm going to buy her a barrel horse."

Rachel laughed. "Sounds like you're the one doing the bribing."

Shane grinned. "Let me get that bucket of chicken and see if I can bribe you out of some barrel-racing lessons for Laura."

It seemed that he could. They sat on the swing and talked and Rachel relaxed, her fears and tears quieted for the moment. The sun dipped in the sky and their voices grew lower in accordance, fading to silence with the last dimming rays....

The faint breeze that passed over the porch was late-evening cool, carrying the soft rustle of green oak leaves, the muffled nicker of the horse in the paddock, the far-off hum of an automobile. As she awoke from the light sleep she'd fallen into, Rachel listened for Rose.

But there was no fretful stirring, no innocent sigh as Rose found her way back to sleep. Rose wasn't here, and Rachel felt the burn of tears behind her closed eyelids; her loneliness wrapped around her like a heavy weight she couldn't escape.

A return to sleep would have been a blessing. But she was awake now.

And she wasn't in bed.

There was the sharp sweet scent of dew on the air she breathed. And the warmer, bolder scent of Shane. Her head rested not on her pillow but in the crook of Shane's left shoulder. His arm was around her and with that realization, the heavy feeling of being held down left her. Rachel found comfort in the weight of his embrace, and more.

Shane's breath warmed her face and she knew his mouth was near hers, knew he wanted to kiss her. She sensed the tension in him, sensed him waiting for her to open her eyes in permission. But that would be like coming out of a dream, facing reality. She couldn't kiss him then....

Shane's lips touched hers gently, soothed the lonely ache in her heart. That was all she wanted, Rachel promised herself, softening her lips in acceptance. Just comfort....

But Shane's kiss was hot and sweet, and she opened her mouth in response, his kiss starting another deeper ache inside her. That ache was tempered by a wariness that had become ingrained in Rachel. When Shane turned her more fully against him, she drew back her hand and levered herself away. Her voice husky, she told Shane, "We can't do this."

Shane tightened his arm around her, then he rested his chin on her hair. Rachel leaned her head on his shoulder. His tenderness made her feel weak, made her long to raise her mouth to his for another kiss. When Shane drew his arm away, Rachel's sigh echoed his.

But Shane's sigh seemed more one of frustration. "We're both adults," he began, but Rachel cut him off quickly.

"That's not reason enough for me." Rachel stared at Shane, at the stubborn set to his shadowed jaw. That he wanted her was clear, as clear as the desire for him that rose within her. It took all the strength she had to refuse him. There were plenty of women who wouldn't have, and she wondered if that same thought was going through his mind now. She was still uncertain of him. And she wasn't about to repeat a past mistake, giving in to lust only to find out she'd misjudged the man. Purposely she reminded him, "We've got the girls to think of."

Shane pushed out of the swing and went to lean against the porch rail. The tense set of his shoulders sent an empty feeling drifting through Rachel. He hadn't gotten what he wanted. He was angry. He was probably going to leave.

"You're right." Shane faced her and Rachel's heart seemed to catch, its next beat hinged on his every word. "The fact is, I don't usually...keep company...with women who have kids. Laura's been hurt by Lana's affairs and I've made it a point not to cause her—or any other kid—pain." Shane gave a wry grin that set Rachel's heart pounding again. "It doesn't help you're so pretty. Guess we'll have to stay out of that swing."

He wasn't apologizing this time. Rachel understood. Shane may have started that kiss, but she'd shared in making it all it had been. The attraction was there, and they both knew it would be a mistake to pursue it.

"I guess we will," Rachel agreed softly.

"Good night, Rachel."

"Night."

Shane went down the porch steps, a cool breeze rushing over his heated skin as he headed toward the trailer. He felt let down and wired up all at the same time, like after a seven-second ride on a bull. One more second and he would have scored....

Shane sighed. Rachel wasn't that kind of woman. He was smart enough to know she meant it when she said that wasn't going to happen between them—not when she had a small daughter depending on her.

Shane thought of how Rose depended on him, too. And he thought of Laura, whose young life was already complicated enough without her coming here to find him involved with a woman who had a child. Like Rachel, he only wanted what was best for his daughter.

At the corner of the trailer, Shane looked back at the porch. Rachel still sat on the swing, rocking gently. She was probably thinking of Rose. He glanced around the ranch and considered Rachel's injured knee and he realized bleakly that on some level, he was already involved. Although it would be an uphill battle with her pride, he knew he would do everything he could to help Rachel for as long as he was here.

# Chapter Six

Summer had set in with a vengeance. Rachel lifted her hat and wiped the sweat from her brow with her forearm before turning the black gelding toward the barn, cutting short his workout for the morning. These past few days she'd battled an aching knee and a simmering attraction for Shane. That effort, combined with the heat, had left her worn and frazzled.

Spending time away from Shane tomorrow at the horse and tack auction north of Guthrie would be good for her—and Rose. She'd readied a client's horse for sale, and the commission she earned would help pay to service her truck. She would have liked to have the brake work done before making the hour's drive, but that simply wasn't an option financially.

Rachel eased her right foot out of the stirrup and let it dangle, resting her knee. She rubbed her neck and felt sweat trickle between her breasts. Her gaze strayed across the sunburned pasture to the front porch where Shane stood watch over Rose.

It had been a long time since she'd had to deal, on a daily basis, with the tension that came from a sexual awareness of a man. Even now, when she ought to be thinking about her horse, she was aware of Shane leaning against a pillar, his denim shirttails teasing her imagination despite the lack of breeze. Because his forehead was still tender, he was hatless, and his shiny black hair drew her gaze repeatedly.

Rachel jerked back her gaze and slipped her foot into the stirrup. All she needed was to be caught unaware again by the gelding beneath her while she daydreamed about Shane. Her pride still stung from being thrown the other day with Shane as witness.

More often than not, when a person got tossed or bitten or kicked it was through their own carelessness. You didn't stick your hand where it might get bitten, you didn't stand where you might get kicked. And you didn't daydream when you were riding a horse that was known to jump at his own shadow. Rachel had to admit her mind hadn't been on her work when the gelding had bucked her off the other day.

Considering that, Rachel thought uneasily of her behavior in the aftermath of her fall. Shane's resentment when he'd slapped down Jace's letter had been clear and his accusation lingered in her mind. Was he right? Did she judge him by Jace's actions? She didn't like to think so.

Hashing over her motives in her mind, Rachel dismounted and loosened the cinch, leading the horse to a hitching post near the water hose that ran from the barn. She traded the gelding's bridle for a halter, pulled off the saddle and blanket and carried them into the barn. She emerged to find Shane headed her way.

He walked slowly to keep pace with Rose's quick but small steps. He carried the yellow-haired doll. That sweet way Shane had with her daughter appealed to Rachel even as it worried her. It was as much a torment as those shirttails and his black hair. He caught her watching him and Rachel went to get the hose, tempted to run the cool water over her head. Maybe she judged Shane by Jace's actions and maybe she didn't. Either way, that didn't change the image she carried of him with those women at Guthrie.

Right now, Shane was coming to give her a hand with the chores, and that knowledge both stirred feelings deep within her and set her on edge. Since she'd hurt her knee, Shane had doubled his efforts to help her regardless of his own injuries. When she'd needed a hand with the wide arena gate, Shane had been there to lift it into place. When a daunting truckload of straw had arrived, he'd hefted bales with one strong arm, which both impressed and frustrated her. All the resulting contact—sweaty bodies brushing, hot gazes meeting and sliding away—had contributed to the frazzled state she was now in.

Rachel directed the hose near the horse and tried to crank the nozzle. It wouldn't budge and frustration swept over her anew. From the corner of her eye she saw Rose take the doll from Shane and run into the barn. She concentrated on the hose. But she could hear Shane's boots scuff the dry ground and felt his approach as if he were inching up her spine. The back of her neck heated and when he reached around her to grip the hose, warmth rushed through her in all directions.

"Let me get that," he instructed, and he tugged at the hose.

Rachel clung tightly to it and faced him, as if by hanging on she kept control not only of the hose, but of the fire running rampant through her. "I can do it."

"Don't be stubborn." Shane sounded impatient. He held fast and Rachel's hand slipped to the nozzle now aimed her way. Water sputtered out in warning.

Apprehension flickered through Rachel.

The nozzle shot off in her hand.

Spray gushed over Rachel and sent the black horse shying sideways. Dust churned from beneath the horse's hooves and settled into the soaked front of her white T-shirt.

"Now look what you've done!" Rachel dropped the nozzle. Then she saw Shane *was* looking and she hastily pulled the now transparent T-shirt loose of her wet bra. A rush rose from her belly to her cheeks and left them burning.

Rose chose that moment to skip out of the barn. At the sight of them, she planted both pink sneakers on the ground. Her mouth popped open.

Shane stared at Rachel long and hard, and it was plain to her in that moment that she wasn't the only one who wrestled with desire. That knowledge seemed to somehow help and at the same time, make matters worse.

"I want to play!" Rose came on the run.

Dropping the hose, Shane caught Rose about the middle and lifted her away from the water. "Whoa, now. Your mama needs that hose. You can go up to the yard and play in your pool."

Fortunately, Rose loved her plastic pool. Rachel felt the heat of one last burning look from Shane before he carted Rose toward the house. Rose grinned over his shoulder all the way to the yard. When cool water seeped through the seams of her old boots, Rachel hopped aside, then grabbed the hose and got back to work, more agitated than ever. Tension dragged out the day for Rachel and restlessness plagued her through the long, lonely night.

The next morning Rachel let Rose play in the barn while she cleaned stalls. She wouldn't be working the horses before leaving for the sale. Aware of her plans, Shane showed up to help, carrying bales of straw and bedding stalls with his good arm. They didn't speak much. Several times she caught his gaze on her. She tried to pretend those miles to the sale were already between them.

Rachel brushed the horse for the sale, then went to get Rose cleaned up and take a quick shower. She'd just finished brushing her hair when Rose called, "Mommy! Shane said I can come outside."

"Rose, wait—" The screen door slammed and Rachel sighed, laying the hairbrush aside. She went to the bathroom window and looked to see Rose and Shane walking toward the barn. Rose carried a red plastic bottle of liquid soap for making bubbles with a wand. Despite her admonishments, Shane was always giving Rose little presents he'd bought on trips into town.

Rachel noticed then that Shane was wearing his hat. The coal-colored Stetson looked good with his black shirt. He'd tucked in the shirttails today. Rachel pursed her lips. The only time he did so was when he went into town. Tucking them in was probably too much trouble with his arm in that cast, but he'd gone to the trouble today and Rachel wondered where Shane was headed. He looked kind of dressed up in that shirt with its fancy pearl snaps and piped yoke.

She'd dressed up a little herself, pairing her favorite white Western shirt, sleeveless with a ruffled yoke, with a white leather belt that threaded through the waist of her newest blue jeans and matched her best leather boots. She'd left her hair loose, except for the sides, which were caught up at the crown in a silver barrette.

Rachel fingered one of the tiny silver horseshoe earrings she wore and watched out the window until Shane disappeared into the barn. Dust lifted and blew from the bare ground in front of the barn's empty doorway. Rachel lowered her hand and turned away.

A minute later she pulled the front door shut, her purse and Rose's doll in hand. She glanced in the direction of the horse trailer parked on the far side of the barn. All she had to do was hitch it to her truck—

Rachel stared. The trailer was already hitched—to Shane's truck. She felt a flutter of anticipation. Was he going to the sale? Rachel chided herself, knowing that was the last thing she needed. She frowned. Shane must have heard the brakes screeching on her pickup. Well, she wasn't using Shane's new truck to haul that horse to the sale. That smacked of charity. Rachel strode to the barn to tell him so.

Once inside, Rachel slowed, struck as always by the sight of Rose doing something memorable. Rose stood before Cash's stall holding the bubble wand in front of the horse's nose. Every time the horse's big nostrils fluttered, bubbles floated about Rose, landing on her red hair bow and drifting to her red boots. Rose giggled. Shane handed her the soap bottle and Rose dipped in the wand for more solution. Too often, of late, Shane was part of the memorable pictures Rachel carried of Rose.

Rose spied her and said, "Mommy, look what Cash can do!"

Rachel laid her purse and Rose's doll on the hay. She walked over and admired Cash's "talent"; the horse stood with his head hung over the stall gate, oblivious to the floating bubbles. Shane's gaze was steady upon her, making her aware of each ruffle across her shirtfront, each strand of hair that escaped to lace her cheeks. Rachel struggled to remember what she'd come in here to say.

Then Shane reached out and touched the ends of her hair where the long strands draped across her bare arm. His knuckles brushed her skin and heat washed over her in waves. Rachel would have sworn she could feel Shane's fingers caressing her hair. Despite everything, she knew this was what she had wanted; for him to admire her hair, her clothes, *her*. Now she realized her folly, and a breathless moment passed before Shane drew back his hand and said huskily, "This horse sale must be a special occasion."

Because she needed him to believe it, Rachel raised her chin and sent her hair sweeping over her shoulder. "The chance to make money is always a special occasion, especially when the feed bill is due."

Shane tucked his hand in his pocket, but the look in his eyes said he wasn't fooled. Drawing a breath, Rachel demanded, "Why is my horse trailer hitched to *your* truck?"

"Because you haven't had a chance to have the brakes on your truck fixed."

Rachel's face heated. She suspected he knew she didn't have the money to pay for repairs.

"It'd be best to have that brake work done before making the trip."

Somehow that observation rankled, coming from someone else. "The brakes on my pickup aren't that bad."

"Are you saying you'd rather drive Rose to the sale in your truck?"

Her pride was stinging now. "No. But we would have gotten by."

"Well, now you don't have to 'get by.'"

Rachel gritted her teeth. If she hadn't been taking Rose along... "I'll pay you for gas and mileage."

"Why would you do that?" Shane was clearly exasperated. "I've still got my horse trailer at the garage, getting the hitch repaired. I thought you could use my truck to drive up there and I could haul Laura's horse back in your trailer."

"Laura's horse?" Before she could stop it, anticipation twirled through Rachel again at the prospect of Shane coming to the sale.

"I told you I want to buy Laura a barrel horse." Shane shrugged. "You're the expert. I figured you could help me pick out the horse."

Shane's offhand recognition of her knowledge was as hard to resist as his touch had been. Imagining the day spent together, Rachel pushed her fingers through her neatly brushed bangs. They'd ride to the sale together in Shane's pickup, Rose strapped in her car seat between them. Once there, he'd be carrying her daughter around while she stood by his side offering advice on which horse to buy. They'd look like a couple to anyone who knew them and rumors would fly. They'd *feel* like a family....

Rachel felt backed against the wall on all counts and she didn't like the feeling. She'd gotten divorced over that feeling. But Shane was right about the truck brakes, and she could hardly say she didn't want him along because she was attracted to him. Mustering what graciousness she could, Rachel muttered, "I reckon I can help pick out a horse."

Shane shifted, causing his shirt to gape and giving her a perfect view of his firm broad chest. That simmering awareness of Shane washed over her in hot waves. It took a moment for his words to sink in when he said, "This trip will be good for us, Rachel."

She looked up at him and she let her doubt show.

"The two of us alone on this ranch, aside from Rose, is leading to some strong temptations. It will do us good to get away from the isolation, spend some time in the company of others."

"Yes..." She'd felt that sense of isolation, that temptation, clear to her soul. But she hadn't imagined them taking time away from the ranch *together*.

"What is it, Rachel?"

"I worry folks will get the wrong impression about us, what with you living out here. I worry word will carry back to Jace. I've been real careful not to give him any excuse to take Rose from me."

"Then I'll be careful, too. I'll make sure no one misunderstands the situation between us. I've got Laura to think of, too."

Because she believed him, Rachel relented. They loaded the horse and got Rose settled in her car seat. Since safety seemed a deciding factor in the turn of events today, and considering Shane's broken arm, Rachel opted to drive. She switched on the ignition, easing the truck down the rutted lane and onto the highway.

Shane settled his left arm across the back of the seat. His fingers brushed her shoulder and Rachel's breath faltered. She couldn't help but worry that her attraction to him would be apparent for all to see. For an instant, his gaze smoldered in her direction and she wondered how anyone would miss *that,* when she could all but feel the heat. She was tempted to turn back home. But as they'd agreed, they needed this time away from the ranch.

Rose wanted the radio on and Shane obliged her, dancing the yellow-haired doll across his lap and delighting Rose. Rachel found his antics both silly and endearing—too much so. She thought how she wouldn't be in this predicament if she hadn't been desperate for someone to watch over Rose.

On the other hand, she'd still be unable to work if Shane hadn't come along. None of the women she'd interviewed this past week to baby-sit Rose had met with her—or Shane's—approval.

Despite Rachel's worries, the hour's drive passed by quickly. Upon arriving, Rachel climbed from the truck and surveyed the fairground where the sale was to be held. With folks milling about and the scent of corn dogs wafting in the air, the place had almost a carnival air that took her back to her days of county-fair rodeos. When she didn't see any familiar faces Rachel relaxed somewhat. She checked in with the sale secretary and Shane helped her stable the horse.

Shane insisted on buying lunch, and, upon learning the rancher's wife running the concession stand was a neighbor of Rachel's, he made a point of saying that Rachel was selecting a barrel horse for his daughter. Rachel appreciated Shane's chivalry on behalf of Rose. She sometimes had the impression that like her, Shane would do anything for Rose.

They'd finished eating corn dogs at a picnic table near the concession stand when Rachel heard a familiar voice call her name. Candy Parker, a petite blond barrel racer Rachel had known since they were teens, came hurrying over, green eyes sparkling.

"Rachel!" Candy embraced her, all but knocking Rachel back to the bench. "Oh, my gosh, is this Rose?" Candy smiled down at Rose. "When I saw you last fall you were just a baby. Now look what a big girl you are!"

Rose beamed. Candy directed a grin at Shane. "Shane Purcell, right? I'm Candy Parker. Folks have been wondering why we haven't seen you around on the circuit. Sorry to see you're laid up with that arm."

Her face lit up. "I didn't realize you were an acquaintance of Rachel's."

"Shane and I met just recently," Rachel said hastily. She loved seeing Candy, but Candy was a romantic, and right now, the gleam in Candy's eyes made her uneasy.

"Rachel's helping me with the purchase of a barrel horse for my daughter," Shane added smoothly.

"Well, I just happen to have one consigned to the sale," Candy said, and to Rachel's relief, talk shifted to the horse.

After a minute, Shane said, "I promised Rose I'd get popcorn. Can I bring you ladies anything?"

"Nothing for me." Rachel caught Rose's free hand while Candy also declined. "I'll keep Rose with me while you stand in line."

Shane nodded and left. Rachel watched after him, only half listening as Candy offered Rose a stick of the peppermint she always carried. But Candy's next words got her attention.

"Wow, Rachel. How'd you lasso Shane Purcell?"

"Shh." Rachel shushed her friend, whose voice seemed to carry clear to Guthrie. "I didn't *lasso* him. I'm helping him choose a horse, just like he said."

"Is he going to have you train it?" Candy sounded hopeful.

Rachel knew Candy imagined wedding bells ringing. Evasively, she replied, "Shane's just keeping the horse at the ranch while he's laid up."

Candy raised her brows. "And where's *Shane* staying while he's laid up? Everybody knows Shane rodeos in Oklahoma to be near his daughter in the summer."

Rachel couldn't bring herself to lie to her. There was no fooling Candy, anyway. "He's renting the trailer Daddy had for the hired hand until he can rope again."

"Oh, wow." The sparkle in Candy's eyes brightened, her imagination apparently off and running.

Rachel caught her lip. This was just what she'd been afraid of.

Candy was a dear friend, but she was also friends with another nine-tenths of Oklahoma. A news bulletin couldn't reach as many people as Candy could in a day, if Candy was of a mind to spread any news.

Maybe Lana had been able to buy her way out of her affairs, but in Rachel's case, Jace was the one who had the money. Taking no chances, Rachel firmly insisted, "It's not like that between me and Shane."

"But, Rachel—"

"The last thing I need is for folks to get the wrong idea, Candy."

Candy sighed her disappointment. "Oh, all right. I know how you worry about Jace. As I recall, Shane's not one to mix with a woman who has a kid, anyway."

Rachel kept silent, knowing the fact that Shane baby-sat Rose would only serve as added fuel to Candy's hyper imagination.

They'd gone back to discussing Candy's horse when Rachel's gaze strayed to Shane. Two attractive cowgirls sidled up to him. To Rachel's amazement, one of them wrapped her arm around his waist, pressing intimately against him to whisper in his ear, right there in front of the concession stand for everyone to see. Shane gave a start, then relaxed with an ease that spoke of familiarity. The women laughed at something Shane said and an angry green haze clouded Rachel's vision.

Candy poked Rachel in the ribs. "All he has to do is stand in one place a minute and the women flock around. Don't pay any attention."

"I'm not paying attention to anything," Rachel said, flustered. She was *glad* Shane was flirting with those women for all the crowd to see, as if she didn't exist, as if he'd never kissed her....

"That redhead hanging on him like a used saddle blanket is Charmayne LaMont," Candy confided. "She thinks she's got a shot at Shane but everyone knows she's the last kind he'd take home to meet his daughter."

Rachel couldn't seem to look away from Shane and the redhead, even when Candy's gaze settled on her with speculation.

"Shane will be probably be bringing his daughter to your ranch this summer. You know, not many cowboys would back off campaigning the way he does to spend time with their kid. That's cost Shane a lot of trophy buckles in calf roping. He's pretty good on the bulls, too, though I hear he only rides them to blow off steam over that no-account ex-wife of his. Take my advice, Rachel. Don't let him get away.''

''I told you, it's not like that. We—''

''Oh, hey, there's Annie and Sue waiting on me. We're headed for Claremore. I'm going to give Wanda Baron a run for third-place standings.'' Candy bent to bestow a kiss on Rose's crown. ''Bye, sweetie.'' She hugged Rachel. ''I'll be back through Guthrie in a few weeks. Maybe I'll see you then.''

''I hope so. . . .''

With a final wave, Candy wove through the crowd, climbed into a bright red rig and was gone.

Rachel sighed, already missing Candy's exuberance in the quiet that marked her friend's departure. She watched Shane and the cowgirls and wondered if what Candy had said was true—that women came on to Shane that way without provocation. Probably they did. But that didn't mean he was above enjoying the good times they offered. Despite herself, Rachel had to envy Shane's resilience after his painful divorce.

''Mommy.'' Rose held up her sticky fingers, her mouth full of peppermint. It seemed a trip to the rest room was in order.

They'd just returned when Shane walked over with the popcorn. He was alone and Rachel turned her attention to Rose in an effort to hide her relief. She watched Rose nibble popcorn from the top of the bag Shane gave her to hold between clean little hands. Rose was going to be sick from all this spoiling.

"I'm sorry I kept you waiting," Shane said, but Rachel noted sourly that he seemed pretty pleased with himself.

"It's no problem. You were talking with friends."

"I agreed to have dinner with Charmayne, the redhead, next time she's in town. I thought it was a nice touch—made it clear you and I were here on business."

That was what Rachel should have wanted to hear, but for some reason Shane's words irritated her no end. "I'll be sure to give you the day off."

"Shoot. A week from now Charmayne won't even remember talking to me," Shane said with a laugh. "Look, she's already hitting on some other fellow."

Rachel looked. Charmayne was indeed engaged in conversation with another cowboy. But Rachel knew better; knew by the way the woman's gaze drifted to Shane that the redhead wouldn't forget a date with him.

"I got this for you."

Shane took a chocolate-chip cookie wrapped in cellophane from his shirt pocket. Rachel loved chocolate-chip cookies.

"It's a *real* cookie. Not that oatmeal stuff."

"I thought you liked my oatmeal cookies."

"I do. But I'll bet you like chocolate chip better, too."

She did. Rachel stared at the cookie, feeling oddly vulnerable, inexplicably touched. It was such a sweet thing to do, bringing her a cookie. Jace had once brought home a diamond necklace for her. But that hadn't seemed as sweet a moment as this.

"Go on. Take it."

Jace had never once given her a cookie....

Rachel took the cookie. "Thank you."

They walked over to the bleachers and sat with Rose tucked between them. When Rachel had finished her cookie, she smoothed the cellophane. She wanted to fold it, to tuck it away in her pocket to save, like a theater ticket or a rose petal she'd been given on a date....

*Foolish woman.* Rachel rose from her seat and excused herself, stepping down the bleachers to walk to the trash barrel and toss the cellophane away. She couldn't so easily banish the cozy feeling that came with thinking that for now, Shane's attention seemed to be for her and Rose alone.

"Faster, Mommy!"

Rounding the third red-striped barrel, Rachel touched her heels to the flanks of Laura's bay gelding. The horse dug in, racing for the gate. Rachel was aware of Rose calling, of her daughter's gold ponytail bobbing from where Rose perched on the fence rail, but her attention didn't waver. She knew Shane stood beside Rose, knew his arm would be wrapped securely around Rose's waist. His whistle shrilled through the air and Rachel grinned, equally pleased with the sturdy little bay Shane had purchased from Candy at the sale a few days ago.

Rachel reined in the horse and looked over at Rose and Shane. Her daughter faced Shane now, her hand raised to his mouth, her fingers trying to purse his lips into another whistle.

"Do that more," Rose demanded.

From over Rose's head and from beneath his hat brim, Shane's gaze sparkled at Rachel. He whistled obligingly—a long, low wolf whistle this time. Rose laughed in delight and Rachel felt her cheeks heat. The day spent at the sale had done nothing to ease her attraction for Shane, while he seemed to have benefited from a day away from the ranch, flirting with those other cowgirls....

Rachel dismounted and loosened the cinch to lead the horse in a walk. From the corner of her eye she saw Shane lift Rose down from the fence and head her way, and she knew her heart beat far too rapidly over a training run at the barrels.

Rose ran to her side. "I want to ride."

The bay stood quietly and Rachel hoisted Rose into the saddle, listening to Shane's boot steps closing in.

"He looked real good today, Rachel." Shane joined Rose in patting the horse's glistening neck.

"That was a pretty sweet run," Rachel agreed. Since the sale, the horse had proved to be all Candy had promised. "Laura's going to be real surprised when she visits this weekend."

"I hope she likes the horse."

Rachel knew Shane's hopes went much higher; knew by the shadow that passed through his eyes that he was thinking of his daughter now, his thoughts reaching beyond this weekend's visit to the two-week stay he hoped would have Laura deciding to remain in his custody. Rachel wished she could reassure him, but she knew all too well there was little reassurance to be offered, no promises to be made.

The phone rang in the barn and Shane reached for Rose. "Come on down, Rosebud. You can ride your tricycle while I walk this horse for your mama."

Rose ran to "barrel race" her trike in the pasture and Rachel handed over the reins. "Thank you."

"You're welcome." Shane smiled. "Better run along before it quits ringing."

Rachel flushed, caught staring at him as the thought ran through her mind that she enjoyed having Shane and Rose hang about while she worked the horse. She stammered a reply and pivoted, heading for the barn before she made a further fool of herself.

Minutes later, Rachel hung up the phone. She leaned against the wall and regarded the scuffed white tops of her boots, pondering the call she'd just taken, the decision she'd made. Raising her hat from her moist brow, Rachel dropped it on a nearby hay bale and walked from the barn to retrieve the horse. She held out a hand for the reins, but Shane only cocked his head in curiosity. "Everything okay?"

"I just took on a client. He's got a green-broke colt he wants trained in the basics."

"Sounds good, especially if he's already got the kinks out of the colt."

"He says he's eventually going to rope off the horse."

"I've seen some of the horses you've been working, Rachel. You'll put a nice handle on the colt for him."

"He says he knows you."

Shane stared at her. Rachel stared back, the warmth of the sun seeming to burn through her.

Shane's jaw took on the stubborn set she'd seen after he'd kissed her on the porch swing. "You got something to say about that?"

She did. But instead, Rachel thought how Jace had never once hung around to watch her ride, had never encouraged her in her work. Now here was Shane, recommending her to a friend, engaging her help with his daughter's horse, doing things with *her* daughter that Jace would never have thought to do. Rachel swallowed hard. Even now, Rose was pedaling hellbent from the pasture to Shane's side.

Rachel grasped the reins from his hand. "Thank you."

She turned and led the horse into the barn, hope rising within her that she was coming to know the real Shane Purcell.

Standing in the bed of her pickup, Rachel tossed the last bale from a load of hay to the barn floor and loosened her faded red T-shirt from her sweat-dampened skin. She didn't need the hand Shane offered to help her jump down. Her knee had mended.

But she shucked her work gloves and grasped his hand anyway, feeling a lot like a child playing with fire.

Her boots landed in line with his and Rachel closed her eyes. The smell of hay and sweat clung to Shane's clothes and skin. His palm was hot against hers. His breath fanned her forehead and she pictured his mouth, imagined it lowering to rest on hers....

Rose's voice came to her from the front of the barn where her daughter played with the kitten. Rachel let go of Shane's hand, opening her eyes. His tanned chest glistened between the unsnapped edges of his denim shirt and she had to swallow hard before she answered, "What is it, Rose?"

"A big car, Mommy."

Shane walked toward the front of the barn and Rachel followed, calling for Rose to stay at the door. Shane turned back with a grin and said, "It's Emma, with Laura!"

Shane strode outside but Rachel halted, dismay racing through her with the early arrival of Shane's daughter—and Emma Blackwell. She'd expected Lana, and she'd expected to be in her house when Lana arrived, with Shane at the trailer. The renter and the rentee.

Rachel strongly suspected Laura's grandmother had arrived early to catch them off guard and assess the situation. Considering Laura, Rachel could hardly blame Emma. If she'd thought Shane's staying here seemed improper, how must it appear to Laura's grandmother? Lana, she suspected, wouldn't have cared.

Brushing the chaff from her jeans, Rachel went to stand at the barn door with Rose. Despite her misgivings, a smile crossed her face.

Clad in jeans, a T-shirt and sneakers, Laura Purcell raced from the Cadillac parked in the drive to fling her slender arms about Shane's neck, all but knocking the hat from his head. He caught her with his good arm and they staggered in a circle, laughing. Rachel met his gaze and shared a grin. *Wait until she sees the horse....*

Emma Blackwell followed from the car more slowly. Her silk T-shirt and long flowered skirt gave her a youthful appearance. But her short dark hair was streaked with silver and her hazel eyes were accented by lines that spoke of years of worry.

Rachel pushed her braid over her shoulder, tucking stray strands behind her ears. Shane was snapping closed his shirt and brushing hay from his jeans. Rachel silently groaned. She and Shane looked like they'd been rolling in the hay.

Shane went to greet Laura's grandmother. Any animosity between Shane and Mrs. Blackwell was carefully masked—for Laura's sake, Rachel was sure.

The three of them started to walk over and Rachel smiled gently at Rose, who stood with one finger in her mouth, solemnly watching their approach. Shane had his arm about Laura's shoulder and Rachel could almost hear Rose wonder how Shane was going to hold *her,* too.

Laura solved that problem, kneeling to admire Rose's kitten. In a moment, Rose was squatted beside her, giving a shy smile.

Rachel waited, unconsciously counting on Shane to smooth the way with introductions. Emma gave him no chance, offering her hand and saying, "I'm Emma Blackwell. Laura's grandmother."

"It's nice to meet you and Laura. I'm Rachel and that's my daughter, Rose." Self-consciously, Rachel wiped her soiled hands on her jeans. "I'm afraid my hands are—"

"Nothing wrong with hard work." Emma grasped her hand as if to put an end to that nonsense. "You've a lovely child."

"Thank you." Rachel relaxed somewhat. With a maturity beyond her twelve years, Laura grinned at her reassuringly.

"I'm sorry for the early intrusion." Emma raised her chin in Shane's direction. "Gus isn't feeling well and I thought it best to bring Laura on out."

"I'm glad to have her," Shane assured Emma. Then, with a concerned glance at his daughter, he lowered his voice to ask with grim resignation, "Where's Lana gone to this time?"

Emma stiffened. "Nevada. She's with . . . a friend, enjoying the casinos in Reno." Laura had gone still at the mention of her mother and Emma's eyes darkened with worry. Tersely she said, "I expect Lana will run out of luck and be home soon."

Shane grimaced and Emma faced the pasture, quickly changing the subject. "Laura will likely enjoy being around these horses."

Rachel felt the brief touch of Emma's gaze and knew she'd been right in assuming Emma wanted to get a look at the place where Laura would be staying. But there was something else there, too. Something familiar. And when Emma glanced at Shane again, Rachel recognized the fear she saw in Emma's eyes. Emma was afraid of losing Laura....

"I'll be going now," Emma said briskly. "Laura, help your dad with your luggage. And please come kiss your grandma goodbye."

But Emma needn't have asked. The girl was already on her feet hugging her grandmother when the words were spoken.

Rose jumped up, too, and Rachel caught her daughter's hand. "It was real nice meeting you, Mrs. Blackwell. Laura, maybe we'll see you after Rose has lunch and a nap."

Emma nodded and Laura smiled. Shane's gaze reflected the warmth Rachel herself had felt each time he'd shown her daughter a kindness.

Rose, however, had caught the word "nap" and sang out a protest, wanting to play with Laura *now*. Rachel lifted Rose, admonishing her not to fuss in front of company. Rose whispered her argument all the way to the house. When she finally settled in for a long nap, Rachel was satisfied. Rose needed rest and Shane needed time alone with his daughter.

It was late afternoon when Rachel pulled on her boots, tied Rose's sneakers, and was ready to go do evening chores. She heard a light knock at the kitchen door. It was Laura.

"I came to thank you for working with my horse." Laura's eyes were round with disbelief even as she spoke the magic words "my horse." "Dad said it's feeding time and I wondered if I could help."

"That's real nice of you, Laura." Rose had been pestering to see Laura since she'd awakened from her nap. Rose was all happy smiles now, as the three of them walked to the barn.

"Dad's putting our supper in the oven," Laura said, and Rachel wondered if the girl could read minds. "He said this weekend is my vacation, but next time when I stay longer, he's going to put me to work."

Rachel doubted that. She suspected Shane had a tendency to spoil his daughter the same as he did Rose.

Once in the barn, Laura went straight to her horse and patted the gelding's nose. Next she lifted Rose to pet him. "Dad told me my horse's name is Tequila."

"That's right. His mama was a champion barrel mare named Marguerita."

"Dad says it's best to stay away from that stuff. Grandma and Grandpa don't approve of drinking, either. They said too much partying has led my mother astray. But I don't think they'll mind if that's my horse's name."

Rachel murmured agreement, her heart going out to the young girl.

They launched into chores then, and when they'd finished, Laura asked, "Could I take Rose to the trailer to play for a while? Grandma helps me baby-sit the little girl next door. She says it will teach me to be responsible when I have a child of my own."

Rachel thought the consequences of Lana's mistakes must weigh heavily on Emma.

"I'll keep a close eye on her. And you can just take a break. Dad said you work hard every day and that you need a break."

"Oh, he did?"

"I did." Shane walked from the door of the barn and was instantly caught by both girls, Laura hugging his arm, Rose his leg. He wasn't wearing his hat and his gaze clearly dared Rachel to take issue with his comment.

But she couldn't take him to task with both girls clinging adoringly to him. Especially when she was thinking what a caring child Laura was—a trait Rachel believed Laura had inherited from her father. Rachel could see where Shane had been driven to dent Lana's fancy car, could understand his need to ride bulls in an effort to blow off steam over Lana.

"Your daddy happens to be right." Rachel ignored Shane's raised brows. "I'd appreciate it if you'd play with Rose at the trailer awhile."

Rose looked at Rachel as if unsure she was truly allowed to go on what sounded like a great adventure. Rachel smiled in permission and Rose clasped Laura's hand, never looking back as Laura led her away. Rachel's throat tightened. Rose was growing up way too fast.

"If you don't feel comfortable about the girls being alone a few minutes I can head on over," Shane offered.

"I was just thinking Rose won't be a baby much longer."

Shane leaned against the gate of Cash's stall. "I was thinking along the same lines. Laura will be a teenager soon. That means lipstick, boys, cars...back seats."

Shane winced and Rachel suspected he'd been well versed in the ways of back seats and women. "Laura seems pretty levelheaded to me."

"She didn't get that from her mama. But I can't fault Gus and Emma. They've taken good care of my daughter."

There was a grudging respect in Shane's voice for the Blackwells despite the part they'd played in Lana gaining custody. Laura's grandparents loved her and Laura obviously returned those feelings. Rachel feared Shane might be disappointed in his hope that Laura would stay with him. That fear twisted in her heart. She didn't want to see Shane hurt....

Still, Rachel said gently, "You're lucky Laura's grandparents care so much for her. I've always suspected if Rose was a boy, Jace's family would have fought for her from birth. As it is, they've never gotten to know her. The same could be said for Jace. All he's had to offer Rose is a rich inheritance—until lately.''

"It's their loss,'' Shane told her, and she knew his words were meant to reassure. "Rose is sweet. A lot like her mother.''

Shane smiled then, and Rachel sought to return both the smile and the reassurance. "I've noticed Laura's a lot like you.''

"Well, she's got my hair.'' Shane's smile turned charming.

"Yes, she does.'' *Dark and silky...*

"And folks are always saying we've got the same eyes.''

*With long, black lashes.*

"I believe she has my smile, too. Just a little prettier.'' Shane grinned.

*So handsome...* Rachel watched Shane's mouth soften, realizing that the flavor of him was indelibly printed upon her tongue. Even as she murmured an agreement, Rachel was reliving his kisses, the warmth and sureness of his mouth on hers.

Shane watched the play of emotions over Rachel's face. He knew her heart was all wrapped up in the hurt Jace had inflicted. But there was feeling for him in her eyes and it made him want to forget the rule that he lived by, to kiss her long and slow the way he'd been wanting to do.

Shane teetered on the edge of that kiss, desire drawing him toward the brink. He had to think of the girls....

Rachel's lips parted on a sigh.

He had to keep his perspective....

Her sweet scent swirled around him.

"Rachel..."

From beyond the barn, the slam of the trailer door reached him.

Shane stepped from the edge of that sweet precipice and said huskily, "Let's go check on our girls."

## Chapter Seven

Shane tossed the red ball to Rose and watched it bounce off her outstretched arms and roll in the grass. He'd given up telling her she had to bend her arms; it just wasn't going to happen. Rose didn't seem to care, chasing the ball with laughing abandon, the way Laura had done at that age.

There was a different ring to Laura's laughter these days. Too often it was wistful, and he could tell her mind was on other things, like her mother. Other times she tried to contain her feelings, probably in an effort to conform to her almost-teenage status. There were times when her attempts were downright indulgent, as if she were humoring her old man. Shane sighed. Somewhere along the way she'd grown up and, somehow, he'd missed it.

Which was probably why he savored the sound of uninhibited giggles when Laura and Rachel walked from the barn. Shane pushed back his hat, struck anew by Rachel's youthfulness—from here in the front yard she and Laura looked like two teenagers with their long flowing hair, flowered shirts and crisp blue jeans.

But Rachel wasn't a child. Shifting his weight to one booted foot, Shane recalled the way Rachel had felt pressed against him the night he'd kissed her in the swing. He still wanted her, and the other evening in the barn that wanting had almost gotten the better of him, even with the girls to consider.

He needed to take care where Rachel was concerned, for Laura had taken to Rachel right off— maybe too much so. He trusted Rachel to be careful with his daughter's feelings in the same way he was careful with Rose. But he worried Laura might come to see Rachel in the light that she should have seen her mother. Where would that leave Laura when the time came for him to leave here?

The red ball bounced off his sling and Shane started, making Rose laugh. Heedless of his good white shirt, he tumbled to the ground, setting off Laura and Rachel, as well. Rose ran and jumped atop him and he lay back in the grass tickling her.

Shane gradually stilled, distracted by the sound of an automobile. Slowly he stood, setting Rose on her feet and handing her the ball. He grimaced. Like an angry green hornet, Lana's sports car sped up the lane.

When it skidded to a stop, scattering gravel into the Indian blanket, Rose raised her arms and Shane lifted her.

His gaze was on Laura, on her sudden quiet and the fall of her slender shoulders.

Rachel met Lana at the edge of the yard. The good witch greeting the bad, Shane thought, the contrast emphasized by Rachel's silky gold hair and Lana's teased black tresses. They came up the walk, Laura trailing behind, aware her visit had come to an abrupt end.

Lana's dark eyes were hidden behind tinted lenses, no doubt to conceal the effects of her weekend in Reno. Still, Shane could feel her gaze drill through him. Rose hugged his neck and he tightened his hold protectively.

"They've certainly been taking good care of you here." Lana's voice was heavy with an innuendo Shane guessed wasn't lost on anyone except Rose. Shane let it pass, hoping Rachel would understand. He'd long ago stopped giving Lana the argument she was always looking for in the presence of his daughter.

Rachel lifted Rose from her perch on his arm. "We'll go inside. Laura, I've got some *Quarter Horse Journal*s in here if you'd like to take them with you."

Laura looked to him, a little girl once again, and Shane sent her on with a nod.

Lana got right to the point. "I've made plans for tonight. This is the only time I have to pick up Laura. Mother will be home to look after her."

"I'll be calling to check on that."

Whatever reply Lana had was interrupted. Laura burst out the door, carrying magazines and a plastic bag of cookies.

"I'm going to the barn to see my horse before I leave."

If anything could have made Shane smile in that moment, it was the authoritative note in Laura's voice. But the smile never came, for he saw the hint of tears in her eyes.

Rachel came out on the porch with Rose. Shane figured they'd already said their goodbyes to Laura when he saw tears in Rose's eyes, too, and a cookie in her hand to soothe her. Rachel told Lana, "You can sit on the swing to wait for Laura if you'd like."

Grateful for a few final minutes alone with his daughter, Shane walked to the barn with Laura. He reminded her of their visit to come. And when she hugged him he held her tightly, pressing his cheek to her hair, storing up her mixed scent of cookies and bubble gum shampoo. They'd planned a cookout tonight before Laura returned home, but Laura didn't fuss over the early departure. She'd long ago learned to compensate for her mother.

Lana was waiting in the car when they came from the barn. Laura wrapped her arms about Shane's neck in one last hug and before he knew it, he was standing in the lane alone, the sports car gone from sight.

Shane clenched his hand and fought the burning in his eyes. God, he hated this. Hated knowing there was nothing he could do to change things that wouldn't hurt Laura more. The emotions spun and twisted inside him and he had no outlet for them, no angry bull to ride.

Shane heard Rachel's light steps behind him. And the urge was strong to turn and take the comfort he knew she would offer; to take all that and more, until he no longer felt the hurt inside him.

"Shane?"

He didn't turn around. Shoving his hat low on his forehead he told her, "I'm going to town."

Shane strode to his truck and climbed in, slamming the door. Rachel understood all too well the hurt he was feeling. If there'd been a bull handy in the pasture, she imagined he would have climbed on. She couldn't help being relieved that he couldn't. But he apparently needed some time alone and she didn't try to stop him as he drove away.

It seemed a long evening. Rose was fussy through supper and their nightly ritual of toothbrushing, stories and prayers. Once in bed she wanted more drinks than was prudent, needed her dolls rearranged by her pillow and repeatedly pulled up her sheet and pushed it down. Although Rose couldn't have put a name to her discontent, Rachel knew her behavior stemmed from her disappointment over Laura's early departure.

Rachel stroked Rose's hair and her daughter finally drifted into an exhausted sleep. She made coffee, washed dishes and folded laundry. She'd often wondered how Shane accomplished such mundane tasks with his arm broken. He had yet to ask for help. But tonight he might need someone to talk to, and Rachel stayed up and dressed, waiting and watching worriedly out the window while the hour grew late.

The clock struck twelve and Rachel's worry took on an edge. By one, she turned out the lamp. There were only so many things a man might be doing at this time of night. She was going to bed.

Rachel marched down the hall to the bathroom and peeled off her clothes for a steamy shower. Vigorously, she shampooed her hair. She closed her eyes and let the water stream over her face. Her efforts were in vain. No amount of soap and water could wash away the memory of the red-haired Charmayne draped over Shane at the sale. Rachel knew, with a numbing certainty, that Shane had sought out Charmayne tonight.

Mechanically, she turned off the faucet and squeezed the water from her hair. Then she heard the sound of truck doors opening and closing outside.

Truck *doors?*

An awful suspicion formed in Rachel's mind, spurring her into action. She yanked a flowered nightshirt over her wet body. She peeked in on Rose, then hurried through the dark house to peer out the kitchen window. Shane's truck was parked near the trailer and she caught the flicker of his white shirttail as he disappeared around the corner. There didn't seem to be anyone else . . .

Rachel hesitated, then the clang of the trailer's metal stairs reached her through the half-open window.

"Let's get to it."

Shane's husky voice came to her with clarity and had the effect of a cattle prod on Rachel. His low, sexy laugh sent her storming from the window to go open the front door. She glared outside, but there were only shadows and silence. Even the crickets had stilled.

Had she heard Shane wrong? Was he only talking to himself? Long seconds of silence passed. Maybe he'd fallen on those stairs.

Rachel pushed open the screen and stepped outside. The murky glow of the yard light fell over the porch and the boards felt cool and damp beneath her bare feet. She'd reached the edge of the steps when she heard a click and the dome light flashed on in Shane's pickup.

Rachel paused. Shane's black hat bobbed inside the truck, then he straightened, shutting the door and heading for the trailer again. He stopped short when he saw her.

Shane stared, and Rachel knew her gown was clinging, the light cast over the porch revealing everything underneath. She should go back inside....

Shane's shirt was unbuttoned and his tanned chest glowed in the mix of lamp-and moonlight. Rachel curled her fingers into her warm palms, certain he could hear her heart pound above the rush of breeze through the oak. Beneath his hat brim, his gaze was dark and inviting and the pull she felt was strong.

When he took a deliberate step toward her, Rachel wanted to take that step, as well.

A paper bag crackled in Shane's hand—the kind of bag the drugstore carried. In that same moment, she heard the trailer door open, saw a light come on inside.

Rachel's nightshirt billowed on the waft of breeze and her moist body cooled. She took a step back. She had a good idea what Shane had bought at the drugstore, knew who waited for him in that trailer.

Shane's glance in that direction only seemed to confirm it. Rachel looked away, her wet hair falling over her shoulder.

"Rachel, wait."

She spun around and went inside, closing the door behind her.

Rachel leaned her back against the frame, thinking Shane wouldn't dare come knocking, praying he might. But his boot steps didn't sound on the porch and Rachel bowed her head.

*The only company I'll be keeping is Laura's.*

He'd *lied* to her. Rachel let the thought consume her.

She'd wasted the whole evening thinking of Shane, worrying over him, when all the while he'd been out with Charmayne....

Rachel pushed away from the door and went to her room. She didn't turn on the light, just flung herself on the bed and lay in the darkness, silently cursing Shane, letting the anger pulse through her.

Her wet hair soaked the back of her nightshirt and after a while, Rachel shivered. She pulled up the sheet, but it didn't help. The coldness seemed to come from within.

Rachel hugged her pillow. Why hadn't Shane talked to her instead of turning to Charmayne for distraction? Tears burned her eyes. When Jace had come for Rose, she'd confided in Shane. He'd comforted her, kissed her....

But now he'd lied to her and Rachel clung to her anger, damned if she'd let a tear fall.

She was still dry-eyed and angry come morning, her head hurting from lack of sleep as she stood beneath the hot sun. She hoisted Rose more securely on her hip, trying to concentrate on the cowboy who leaned against her pasture fence, carrying on about the horse he'd just hauled in. Rachel remembered him vaguely from earlier days, when she'd rodeoed with Candy and Annie and Sue. He remembered her, too, and the glint in his eye made it clear that he'd like to get better acquainted.

But with the opening of the trailer door, Rachel's gaze shot past the cowboy's shoulder. Shane trod down the stairs and Rachel's heart caught as she waited for Charmayne to appear behind him.

Shane walked over alone. He was still wearing his white shirt unbuttoned and revealing his bare chest, his jeans slung so low on his hips that the cuffs pooled on the tops of his boots. A night's growth of beard shadowed his jaw and his disheveled hair swept across his frowning forehead—as if *someone* had combed their fingers through it. Rachel glared back at him, irritated by the weak, fluttery feeling his approach gave her.

Rose demanded to be put down. Because she wasn't up to an argument with a headstrong three-year-old, Rachel set down her daughter, pursing her lips when Rose ran to greet Shane.

"About you training my horse—"

Rachel turned a blazing smile on the waiting cowboy. "Why don't you unload him and let him have a roll in the pasture. I'll just be a minute, then we can talk."

"You bet, honey."

The cowboy swaggered away and Rachel grimaced. *Men.* They all thought they were God's gift when they were really a pain in the—

"Mommy, Shane gave me sugar."

Rachel turned to see Shane pat Rose on her jeans-clad bottom. "Go give that to Cash, Rosebud."

Oblivious to the tension overhead, Rose galloped to the barn. Her daughter's easy compliance with Shane's command only added to Rachel's pique. She folded her arms across her middle and waited to see what he had to say for himself.

"Do you know who the hell that cowboy is?"

Rachel bristled; Shane's demand was not at all what she expected. Although she couldn't remember the cowboy's name, Rachel snapped, "Of course, I do."

"Then why have you got him unloading his horse? He's the biggest womanizer on the circuit."

Rachel let out her breath in a huff. "You should talk."

"What's that supposed to mean?" Shane demanded.

"As if you don't know." She wouldn't be fooled by that righteous spark in his eyes.

Shane seemed to hesitate. "Look, I know you're mad about last night, but—"

"If you're only going to make excuses, I don't care to listen."

Shane ran his hand over his face, his exasperation evident. "Fine. But hear me on this—that cowboy's just looking to try you on, Rachel. Steer clear of him."

"That's crude."

"So's he."

"And what do you call bringing your—"

Rachel cut off midsentence. A haggard-looking cowboy had come out the trailer door. He stumbled when another cowboy pushed out behind him. Then another.

It went without saying that the three bowlegged cowboys who moved like they wore tight Ace bandages under their shirts and ached in every bone of their body were bull riders. Rachel drew a deep breath. *Shane hadn't spent the night with Charmayne....*

"I got in a card game with them last night. When the tavern closed, we moved the game here—just me and the boys," Shane added, his gaze black enough to let her know she'd better get that point clear.

"Hey, Shane," one of the bull riders called. "You got all my money. Don't expect me to call a cab, too."

"I'll be right there." Shane's mouth was grim. "I've got to run those guys back to Guthrie. You'd do well to get that cowboy out of here before I go."

At the sight of the bull riders Rachel had thawed toward Shane, but his words frosted her over again— not a hard thing to do after a night of worry and little sleep. "I think I can make that decision for myself."

Shane's nostrils flared. "Then I'll leave you to do just that."

He stomped across the yard, his shirt billowing behind him. Rachel stared after him, breathing hard, giving a start when Rose clutched her leg.

"Where is Shane going, Mommy?"

"He's taking his friends home."

One cowboy got in the cab, the other two climbed in the bed of the pickup. Shane wheeled the truck around and lit for town, leaving Rachel with a whining daughter and a leering cowboy to attend to.

But she stood rooted in the sun, watching the dust churn and settle in the lane, her anger with Shane fading. Oh, he'd broken his word, all right. But faced with the evidence of how he'd spent the night, she felt the coldness ease out of her heart. The worrisome truth settled in that it was the thought of Shane sharing a bed with another woman that had upset her.

"Mommy, I'm tired."

Rachel smoothed Rose's hair. "So am I. Let's help that cowboy load his horse back up and then we'll take a nap."

That was how Shane found them, taking their nap. Through the screen door, he could just see Rachel's hair spilling over the couch, Rose's head tucked beneath her chin.

Rose stirred and Rachel opened her eyes, looking at him. Shane let himself inside and crossed the floor, careful not to scrape his boots on the hardwood finish. He knelt beside the couch and remembered the way he'd napped there with Rose, how he'd kissed Rachel when he'd awakened.

She smelled the same as she had that day, like sunshine. But in his mind he saw her standing on the porch in the moonlight, her feet bare, her gown lifting on the breeze, then molding to her soft curves, her long hair falling over her shoulder. . . .

"I'm sorry about last night." Shane kept his voice low.

"It's okay. I was angry, but now—I understand."

"I just needed to blow off steam. I drank a few beers, played some poker. I guess I just didn't want the game to end, didn't want to be alone."

"I waited up for you. In case you needed to talk."

It wouldn't have been enough just to talk to Rachel, Shane thought grimly. "I shouldn't have gone drinking and gambling or brought those guys out here."

"But you couldn't find a bull to ride and you had to do something."

"That's right." But he would rather have held her, would rather have made love to Rachel the way he wanted to do now. It didn't help, knowing that for a moment last night in the moonlight, she'd wanted him, too.

Rose snuggled more closely to Rachel and Shane got to his feet. He'd made his apologies and Rachel had been forgiving, but he still felt strangely downhearted. "You and Rose sleep. I'll check on the horses."

"Thank you." Rachel smiled sleepily. "I didn't take on that cowboy's horse. He had too many bad habits."

"So did that cowboy."

Shane grinned, his spirit lifting, and the good feeling carried him through the days that followed. He and Rachel fell back into pattern, Shane watching Rose while Rachel rode, he and Rose wandering over to get in the way sometimes. Rachel didn't seem to mind.

Two weeks passed until the day came that he was to pick up Laura in the late afternoon for her extended visit. Shane waited out the morning, then walked with Rose to the barn. He'd taken to turning out Cash in the pasture once Rachel was finished training. Rachel stood with him now and they leaned on the fence and watched Cash roll in the dust—a complete rollover, as only the best horses do. Shane was pleased with how well the horse had mended. Cash had a scar, but on his plain brown hide it seemed almost a mark of beauty.

Shane was mending, too, and he was especially relieved by the flex in his hand that indicated less damage than anticipated. A trip to the doctor had confirmed that. But as he stood in the hot sun and swirling dust, Shane didn't think once about throwing an accurate loop.

He thought about how, if his hand didn't mend well enough to compete, he wouldn't mind having a ranch down this way near Laura, where he could train roping horses. A ranch was hard work, but Rachel was making a go of it here.

He looked down at her then, the sun sparking off her hair, her scent rising sweetly above the pungent smell of horse and the swirling dust. Her small hand was curled on the fence, somehow managing to look both feminine and strong, a combination that pushed all thought from Shane's mind but how it would feel to have both his hands to hold her.

It was a thought he couldn't drown, not even when he went to take a shower, for the shower broke down. Shane tinkered with the fixture, but after a half hour of sweating and swearing, he realized the situation called for more than any makeshift repairs he could manage. He could buy a new fixture in town. For now, he would have to request the use of Rachel's shower.

Shane gave her a call, then grabbed some clothes and his shaving kit and headed over to the house, just as she'd invited him to do. Rachel met him at the door, pressing a finger to her soft pink lips.

"Rose is napping. You'll have to be quiet. I'm real sorry for the inconvenience."

"I think that's my line." Shane stared at her mouth, clenching his hand on the bundle he carried. The trouble was, he didn't feel inconvenienced at all. Rachel had apparently just come from the shower herself, for her hair was damp and glistening and hanging down her back. She'd traded her jeans for a sleeveless denim dress; her feet were bare like they'd been that night on the porch. Shane dragged up his gaze from Rachel's trim ankles. "I'll stop at the hardware store while I'm in Guthrie. Laura can help me make repairs when we get back."

"I'd appreciate that. I'll give you a check to take with you for the parts."

Her voice was firm and Shane didn't argue. He'd come up against Rachel's pride often enough lately. It would be best to let it go this time and save his argument for a more important issue. With Rachel, one was sure to come along.

Shane pried off his boots and Rachel led the way down the hall to the bathroom. "There are plenty of towels in the cupboard. Just help yourself."

"Thanks, Rachel."

Shane closed the door behind him, shutting her out, only to be assailed by the lingering scent of her from her shower. The room was blatantly feminine, which wasn't surprising with only females living in the house.

On the counter was a tortoiseshell hairbrush, with a smaller pink brush beside it. Rachel's silver barrettes were clustered in one trinket box, Rose's hair bows in another. Shane stared a long moment at the combination of his black comb lying beside their things.

There was a small bucket of Rose's toys on a step stool, and in the tub, a naked doll whose hair had seen better days. Setting the doll aside, Shane stripped and showered quickly, taking care not to get his cast wet and relishing the breeze that fluttered the curtains on the window. When he was finished, he grabbed one of the pink towels from the cupboard, swiping it across his chest and over his hair. The whole bathroom was pink and cream, and it reminded him of Rachel. He could picture her standing in front of this mirror, her skin beaded with moisture from her shower, while she brushed her long, damp hair. A toothpaste smudge low on the mirror altered the image, and he grinned, picturing Rose standing on the step stool, brushing her tiny white teeth.

Voices drifted through the window. Someone was on the porch talking with Rachel. Lowering the towel, Shane went to draw closed the curtain, although the window was set past the porch and he doubted anyone could see in.

One of the voices grew louder and Shane stilled at the angry male tone.

"Elizabeth . . . can't conceive . . . want Rose. . . ."

*Jace Callahan.* Shane's hand fisted about the lacy cream curtain.

"Purcell . . . sleeping here . . ."

Shane cursed beneath his breath. Jace was threatening Rachel with *him*.

"Your addiction . . ."

"No . . . you can't. . . ."

Shane dropped the towel to the floor. Thoughts flashed through his mind of the threats Lana had made, how her family had helped fulfill them. If Jace managed to sully Rachel's reputation, and started harping on her past addiction, the oilman might have case enough to gain custody. Jace sure as hell had the money to try.

And this was a hell of a time to be caught with his pants down. Shane grabbed his jeans and stumbled into them, yanking them up his wet legs and struggling with the zipper. With a final curse, he ran barefoot from the bathroom, shirt and sling forgotten in his rush through the house.

Shane pushed open the screen door and strode out. Some instinct reminded him to catch the door to keep it from banging and waking Rose, and that action served to slow the adrenaline pumping through him, to keep his temper in check. Still, Rachel looked at him with wide eyes and Jace hesitated midsentence. Taking an immediate dislike to the wealthy oilman with the styled brown hair, cool blue eyes and three-piece suit, Shane said grimly, "Is everything okay, Rachel?"

Jace recovered quickly then. Taking deliberate note of Shane's wet hair and lack of shirt, Jace told Rachel smugly, "I rest my case."

Riled again, Shane stepped forward, but Rachel blocked his way, frowning at *him* before she spun to tell Jace, "You don't have a case."

Shane set his jaw and wished he'd thrown on his shirt.

"Shane, would you please tell my ex-husband what you're doing here on my ranch?"

Talking to Jace wasn't Shane's first instinct. But he'd learned the hard way to vent his temper on the back of a bull, and Shane took a mental eight-second ride, the angry haze clearing enough that an idea came to mind. Wrapping his arm about Rachel's trim waist, Shane fitted the curve of her hip to his side and with amazing ease he lied, "I'm spending time with my fiancée."

Rachel gasped and Shane felt her body tense. He gave her a warning squeeze.

Jace's nostrils flared. "You two are engaged?"

"Yes."

"No!"

Shane grimaced. "She's just giving me a hard time until I get her the ring."

"Shane!"

"See what I mean?"

Rachel glared up at him, her cool silky hair brushing his bare skin from his chest to his belly. Shane's mind went blank on a moment of pure pleasure and he tightened his arm around her. Rachel dug her fingers into his hand, but he held steady, his heart drumming with his awareness of her.

Jace clenched his jaw. "I guess congratulations are in order. But at the risk of revealing your less-than-sterling qualities, Rachel, I'll remind you again that your past drug addiction is enough to allow me custody of Rose."

His patience at an end, Shane let go of Rachel and stepped between her and Jace. "The only thing Rachel's addicted to now is her fiancé."

Rachel grasped his fisted hand with both of hers and Shane was sure he was in store for another one of her disapproving glances. But she only said, "Jace, I want you to leave."

Jace was already headed down the porch steps. "I'll be talking to my lawyer, Rachel."

"I'll be talking to mine," Rachel retorted.

Shane felt a grim satisfaction as Jace's hasty exit caused the flying gravel to chip at the oilman's luxury sedan. He breathed deeply though his nostrils, adrenaline still pumping through him and a warm sensation building where Rachel's palms cupped his hand.

"Are you crazy?"

Rachel released him and the sensation cooled abruptly. Shane braced himself. Here was the issue he'd saved his argument for.

"You didn't have to tell Jace we're engaged!" Rachel's breath hissed over his naked chest. "You only had to say you're renting the trailer. I could have handled the rest myself."

Her words pricked at something inside him. "It seemed to me you needed a little help."

"That's for *me* to decide, not *you*."

Rachel's slender finger poking his chest torched any remaining patience Shane had. He grabbed her hand and backed her against the house, keeping her arm trapped between them. "Dammit, Rachel. Jace isn't making threats this time. His wife can't conceive. He's going to take Rose."

"*If*. He said *if* his wife can't conceive, he wants Rose."

Rachel's words settled in with the intensity of the hot sun that burned his bare back.

Something uncoiled within Shane, allowing him to think, for the time being, that Rose was safe. Guilt rode on the heels of that feeling as Rachel gazed up at him in defiance. He'd backed her against the wall, literally and figuratively, the way he suspected Jace must have done in the past.

Shane let go of Rachel—not an easy thing to do with her scent swirling between them. Strands of her hair were caught in his fingers and he let them slip free, turning to look out over the yard, letting the breeze cool him.

From the corner of his eye he saw Rachel push her hand through her hair. In a tremulous voice she said, "I thought you were going to hit Jace."

"I wanted to." He hadn't been so angry, so frustrated in years. Not since Lana had taken Laura from him.

Shane could sense Rachel watching him. After a moment she said softly, "It's not your fight."

He faced her. "I feel like it is. I feel like I want to protect Rose in the same way that I want to protect Laura."

His words hung in the air between him and Rachel with all their implications. Shane saw her weigh them in her mind, although she kept her thoughts to herself. His own mind was churning with the ramifications of what he'd said. But the words had felt right, and he let them stand.

"Jace won't keep quiet about the engagement," Rachel finally said.

"Maybe not. I still say the engagement is to your advantage—and Rose's," Shane said stubbornly.

For a moment, Rachel looked stubborn, too. Then her gaze wavered down the lane after Jace and she murmured, "I don't really have a lawyer."

"If we handle this right, you won't need one."

"You're right," Rachel admitted wearily. "Jace backed off after you told him. But, Shane, what if Laura should hear we're engaged?"

"I'll tell Laura myself. She's old enough to understand that we're trying to protect Rose."

"If you're sure."

"I'm sure." He was damn sure about this whole charade. He wasn't going to let Rachel stand up to Jace alone.

Rachel sighed. "This isn't going to be easy, especially if word gets out."

"It isn't going to be easy for a whole lot of reasons," Shane said wryly. "Like I told you before, it would help if you weren't so pretty."

Rachel caught her lip, watched his eyes follow the movement. It would help if *he* weren't so charming, his wet hair not so black and shiny, his jaw not so smooth, his chest not so sleek and firm. The smell of soap and shampoo—her shampoo—clung to him, and Rachel thought of how long it had been since she'd beheld a man fresh from the shower, looking at her the way Shane was looking at her now. She had to remind herself that Jace had once looked at her that way, too.

"I'd better go finish up inside," Shane said, and Rachel could have sworn he'd known the moment her thoughts had turned to Jace.

Shane went into her house, leaving her standing in the warm summer air. Rachel curled her bare toes on the porch boards, her heart full of yearning, her mind filled with uncertainty.

## Chapter Eight

"**Y**ou're going to have to kiss Rachel."

Laura's clear sweet voice hung in the sultry evening air as she addressed Shane from her perch on the porch step. Rachel juggled the tray of iced glasses of lemonade she carried from the house, aware Shane had brought the swing to an abrupt halt. They'd been relieved by Laura's acceptance of their plan, but Rachel hadn't expected this wholehearted support.

"People won't be convinced unless you act like you're in love," Laura told Shane earnestly, and it was clear she'd given the matter some thought. "Don't you think so, Rachel?"

Rachel set down the tray and wiped her moist hands on her denim dress, grateful Rose played in the yard, out of earshot. But Rachel could feel Shane's penetrating gaze when she answered, "We shouldn't have to actually *kiss* one another."

"But people who hear of the engagement, then see you and Dad together, will expect some romantic stuff," Laura insisted. Her expression brightened. "Grandma's always telling me about the 'good old days,' how Grandpa kissed her and gave her flowers. I can coach you in all the stuff Grandma and Grandpa did during their courtship."

"You'd better let us think about this," Rachel said with a meaningful glance at Shane. "I'll do just that while I wash the dishes.

"I can do them," Laura offered, rising from the step.

"That's nice of you, Laura, but this is your first night here. You should spend it with your dad." Certainly Shane would take this opportunity and speak with Laura about the romantic aspects of their "engagement."

"Okay. I'll keep an eye on Rose. And thank you for supper. I love fried chicken."

"You're welcome." Rachel smiled and went inside to the kitchen. Laura was such a sweet girl. She had worried that even a pretense of a relationship between her and Shane might upset Laura. Now she was worried Laura might get too caught up in the "courtship," with talk of flowers and kisses. . . .

Rachel rested her hand on the bottle of dish soap and stared out the window, romantic images floating through her mind. She closed her eyes and could almost feel Shane's lips brush hers, hear his husky voice. . . .

"So you can see that while this engagement isn't real, it isn't a game, either. The court gave custody of Rose to Rachel, but Jace wants to change the judge's mind."

Rachel blinked, as the breeze that ruffled the kitchen curtains played over her face carried Shane's voice from the porch.

"I don't think Rose would like that," Laura said with an insight that surprised Rachel, given how Laura so obviously missed her own father during their separations. "She never talks about Jace but she's always saying things about Rachel."

"We don't think it would be best for Rose, either. That's why we're pretending to be engaged."

"So no one will think you and Rachel live in sin," Laura said sagely, and Rachel cupped her hand over her mouth to stifle a gasp. "That's what Grandma calls living together."

There was a pause and Shane asked, "Grandma doesn't think that of me and Rachel, does she?"

Rachel held her breath in anticipation of Laura's answer.

"Oh, no. Grandma would have said so. She always says what's on her mind. She tells me I should, too."

"She's a pretty smart grandma," Shane observed and Rachel silently agreed. But she could hear Shane's regret over Grandma being the one to instill that characteristic in his daughter.

"I know the court usually gives custody of kids to their mother, like the judge did with me." Laura's statement was a little muffled, as if she'd bowed her head. Rachel peeked out the window. Shane had joined Laura on the step, his head bowed, too.

"I guess the judge knew what a great grandma and grandpa you'd get with the deal." Shane's tone remained light, but Rachel sensed the effort behind each word.

"I guess so. But it doesn't seem right that a judge decides what a kid should do. They ought to just ask kids where they want to live."

"That's a big decision to make. Rose is still too young to decide for herself."

Rachel could almost see Shane's words being absorbed by Laura in the silence that followed. She thought maybe Shane was setting himself up for heartache.

"Am I still too young?" There was only a trace of hesitance in Laura's question, little hint that the course of her future could be affected by Shane's answer.

And although his every prayer was hinged on Laura's response, Shane didn't miss a beat when he told her, "You're old enough now to decide for yourself."

Rachel gripped the edge of the sink in the long silence that followed. She knew Shane would never pressure Laura, knew Laura was indeed old enough to be aware a choice existed. But it was hard to see where someone wasn't going to come out of this situation hurt.

"Did you ever just wish I lived with you instead, Dad?"

Shane reached out his hand and smoothed Laura's hair the way Rachel had seen him do the night of the fair. In a low soft voice she knew hid a wealth of pain and regret, he told Laura, "Every day of your life."

It was apparently the right answer. Laura hugged Shane about the neck with both arms. Shane folded his arm around Laura more slowly, as if he already knew she would be impossible to hang on to.

Rachel blinked her moist eyes, frustrated to think there was nothing she could do. But then, there was always a price to pay for eavesdropping. She watched Laura run to play with Rose, saw Shane lean against the porch rail, and felt the burden of her helplessness settle in her heart.

The first two days of Laura's visit centered on spending time with the horses. Laura had learned to ride on Cash. Her natural ability and enthusiasm, combined with instruction from Rachel, had her successfully turning the barrels on Tequila in no time at all.

In the evenings, the four of them seemed to gravitate to Rachel's front porch where she and Shane would watch the girls play. A part of her warned that once Shane and Laura were gone, Rose would miss their companionship. She didn't want to think about how lonely the ranch would seem without them. Still, when the need to visit the tack shop came, Rachel thought it prudent for her and Rose to make the trip alone. Rose didn't agree.

Rachel shut the front door and caught Rose's hand before her daughter could go running to the trailer.

Rose tried to pull free. She stomped her pink sneakers on the porch and the ruffle on her denim skirt bounced. "Mommy, I want Laura to come!"

Rachel pushed her unbound hair from her face, her blue-flowered dress already sticking to her back from the heat as she struggled to calm Rose. Dropping her purse, Rachel knelt to Rose's level. "You and I will have fun together, Rose. We'll have ice cream after Mommy buys the supplies she needs."

Rose stopped jumping, and her earnest expression made Rachel feel guilty. "I want fun with Laura, too."

"Laura will want to stay with her dad. I promise you can play with her when we get back."

Rose's face puckered, and she wavered between tears and anger. The stubbornness Rachel hoped would someday prove a strength, darkened Rose's eyes. Any hope Rachel had that Rose might cooperate was fading fast. It vanished completely when Shane and Laura walked around the corner of the trailer.

"I want Laura!"

Rose stomped again and one pink sneaker came down hard on Rachel's sandaled foot. Rachel sank to the step, rubbing her arch, and Rose wiggled free, running across the yard to Laura and Shane. Rachel heard Rose's little-girl voice tattling on her and she sighed. This was going to be a long day.

Shane had braced his hand on one knee to listen. He nodded as if he understood Rose's predicament and possibly sided with it. When he straightened, he pushed back his hat and grinned at Rachel.

Rachel pursed her lips. She didn't find the situation funny.

But as Shane talked with the girls, Rachel's irritation took a provocative slant. He was wearing another of those sexy black shirts, this one with a weave of turquoise across the yoke. And the tails were tucked into black jeans that covered the tops of shiny black boots. Rachel rested her hand about her ankle. Even with his arm lying across his chest in a sling, a woman could easily imagine herself pulled against Shane's tall lean body in a slow dance.... Or on a soft bed...

Shane looked at her then, his gaze lingering on her legs, although the skirt of her dress draped demurely over her knees. An alluring warmth stole through Rachel, enhancing the seductive image in her mind.

Rose giggled, dispelling that image, and covered her mouth with her hands, the way she did when trying to keep a secret. Rose loved secrets.

But Rachel had a feeling *she* wasn't going to like this one. Laura was dressed in clean jeans and a good pink Western shirt—which probably pleased Rose, who also wore pink, and which made it easy for Rachel to guess that Shane was going to Guthrie, also.

The girls ran for Shane's truck and he crossed the yard, planting one booted foot on the step. "Looks like we're all headed in the same direction."

"Rose and I are only making a quick trip to the tack shop," Rachel said quickly. "It might be best if we each drove in."

"There's no need. I'm taking Laura to get new boots. We may as well go together."

"Oh." For all the wrong reasons, Rachel's heart leaped at his words. Over in Shane's truck, Rose was pretending to drive, laughing at something Laura was saying. Rachel ought to remind Shane of her concerns over Rose. But he would only reassure her that Rose wouldn't be hurt when he and Laura left them....

"Are you worried about coming across Jace in town?"

"No." Rachel smiled dryly, then. "Jace was never one to visit the tack shops. But Jace knows a lot of people in Guthrie. There is a possibility that he's already spread word around of the engagement. It could be real awkward, the two of us running into someone Jace and I know."

"It could help where Rose is concerned," Shane reminded. "And there's a chance our engagement won't even come up. Laura will be there to coach us if it does," he added teasingly.

"That's not funny," Rachel said primly. Leaning close, clean-shaven and smelling of spice, Shane didn't *need* any coaching. Rachel wavered in her resolve. She wanted the four of them to go to town together. It would make Rose happy. It would make her happy....

"Come on, Rachel. The girls will have fun. And I don't know about you, but I'm in need of another day away from this ranch."

His dark gaze flicked over her with his words, and there was no mistaking his meaning. Shane held out his hand and Rachel's heart fluttered, the yearning he'd planted within her deepening. Shane made her wish for things she'd finally learned to live without. Rachel took his hand anyway.

Although she'd never been content in the fine big house Jace owned in Guthrie, Rachel had always liked the quaint historical community. By the time they'd arrived at their chosen tack shop, the girls' good humor had taken a hold of Rachel. She needed some liniment and fly spray for the horses, but helping Laura choose new boots just naturally drew her.

Shane wanted to buy Rose a pair of boots, also. Rachel didn't feel right about that. While the girls pulled on an array of different style boots, she told him, "It's too expensive a gift."

Shane said patiently, "They aren't too expensive."

"Rose has a pair of boots at home."

"Now she'll have two pair."

"She'll outgrow them before she can wear them out."

"How about pink boots?" Shane motioned to a tiny pair and Rachel thought how cute they would look with Rose's denim skirt. Then she thought what a picture she and Shane must make, standing over the pink-clad girls, arguing about the price and wear of boots.

The store clerk, an old acquaintance, was watching with an indulgent smile, and two elderly customers were blatantly eavesdropping while they enjoyed the girls' modeling of boots. Bells rang as the store's front door opened and Rachel averted her gaze, feeling as if all of Guthrie had come to observe the foursome they made.

A silver-haired man checking out a display of turquoise at the counter caught her attention with his pin-striped suit and tie. Rachel's breath lodged in her chest. She knew him. And he knew Jace.

Rachel inched closer to Shane and unconsciously clutched his shirtfront. "That man over there—he's a lawyer friend of Jace's."

She tried to recall the man's name and more important, his status. Was he one of the lawyers Jace's family dealt with who had connections in the courts?

Rachel was suddenly aware of Shane's lack of response, his stillness. And she realized how close she stood to him, his breath coming softly between his parted lips, his eyes glowing down at her. His heart beat intently against the back of her hand.

Rachel let go abruptly. After a moment, Shane looked over his shoulder.

"There's a guy in a suit coming this way."

"That's him." Rachel drew a shaky breath. She and Shane stepped apart, but only slightly, for Shane slipped his arm about her waist in a way that was both natural and stirring. Rachel thought their pose must be convincing to the man approaching.

"Rachel Callahan." The man offered a hand. "Howard Latham. We met when I worked with Jace on the purchase of a well years ago."

"I remember you, Mr. Latham." He still had the same cold handshake and phony smile.

"Call me Howard, please. And this must be your fiancé. Jace and I are working on another venture and he's spoken of your recent engagement."

Rachel's throat felt parched. She was aware Laura had paused and was listening. She hated lying, even to this sly lawyer. But Shane extended his hand and said smoothly, "I'm Shane Purcell."

Rachel felt bereft without Shane's arm about her. Howard reminded her of a circling hawk, just waiting for her to make a mistake, to expose the lie so he could carry the news back to Jace. She felt his gaze skim her bare ring finger.

"Have you chosen a wedding date?" With Howard's words, the store's doorbells jangled in mockery.

Rose danced happily in her stocking feet, waiting to try on another boot. Rachel wanted to gather up Rose and warn Howard there was nothing he could do to help Jace gain custody of their daughter.

Instead, she went lax against Shane's side, bringing her bare left hand to rest on his belly below his sling. His stomach was flat against her palm and Rachel sucked in a breath. She put on a smile for Howard and drawled, "We hope to set a date real soon."

Shane pressed his hand to the small of her back. The muscles of his belly grew taut beneath her fingers. His gaze blazed down on her.

"I knew it!"

Startled, Rachel turned to find Candy swinging the store door shut, setting those damned bells off again.

"I knew you two would wind up setting a wedding date!" Candy grinned as she crossed the store.

Rachel shot Shane a strained smile and saw the heat slip from his eyes, to be replaced by a composure she struggled to copy. Howard was watching. Everyone was watching....

Candy caught her hands in a quick squeeze. "I'm so happy for both of you!"

"If you'll excuse me," Howard put in, "I've a purchase to make. It was a pleasure to see you, Rachel. Shane." Howard gave a nod and returned to the counter.

"Could you give the girls a hand with those boots?" Rachel asked Shane. She couldn't handle any more pretense with him right now. Shane hesitated, then tipped his hat to Candy and went to help the girls.

Rachel braced herself. She didn't like deceiving Candy, but there was too much at stake to risk Howard overhearing the truth. Even now, he edged their way, moving within earshot along the counter.

"Darn." Candy sighed. "There's a million things I want to ask you, but like always, I'm in a hurry. An-

nie's waiting for me in the truck. We left Sue in Claremore with *her* fiancé and Annie wants to get to
Amarillo and meet up with her boyfriend. They're on
the verge of tying the knot, too. Seems like everyone's getting married these days."

There was a wistfulness to Candy's voice that Rachel felt echo within her. "I wish we could talk some-
time, Candy."

"Next time I'm passing through, I promise." Candy
smiled over at Shane and the girls. "You and Shane
seem so right for one another." Candy gave her a hug
that smelled of peppermint and horses and made Rachel recall a less complicated time in her life. "I've got
to grab a pair of Wranglers and run. I'll say hi to Annie for you."

Candy spun away, snatching up a pair of jeans and
making a hasty purchase before hurrying out the door.
Rachel thought of how as teens she and Candy had
had the same dream—to find the right man and marry,
to have a family. But Candy hadn't found the right
man yet and Rachel had married the wrong one. She'd
given up on the idea.

Until lately. Rachel turned toward the girls. Shane
knelt before Rose, who sat in a chair, her arms resting
on the sides, her legs stuck straight out on the seat.
With his good hand, Shane slid a small pink boot over
Rose's frilly sock. When the other boot was in place,
Rose waggled her feet and smiled at him with adora-
tion. Rachel felt that mix of hope and worry that had

become familiar to her since Shane's arrival at the ranch.

"Ready to go?" Shane asked, rising and lifting Rose off the chair. Laura wore new boots, also. It seemed the girls were indeed ready. Skirting past Howard, the four of them collected Rachel's supplies, made their purchases and left the store.

Helping Shane set Rachel's box of supplies in the bed of the truck, Laura said with conviction, "That man didn't believe you and Rachel are going to get married. He saw Rachel wasn't wearing a ring."

Rachel caught Rose's hand to keep her from prancing near the curb in her new boots, then glanced through the store window to catch Howard looking away.

Rachel had thought she was pretty convincing, draped all over Shane the way she'd been. Even Candy had seemed, inadvertently, to add credence to their story. But now, Rachel wasn't so certain.

"You're right, Laura," Shane answered grimly. He pulled some money from his jeans pocket and handed it to Laura. "Why don't you take Rose down the street to that ice-cream parlor? Rachel and I will be right along."

Before Rachel could ask what Shane had in mind, Rose jumped up and down, full of excitement now at the mention of ice cream. "Am I going with Laura?"

"If you promise to hold Laura's hand," Shane said.

"I'll hold her hand," Rose promised.

And she did, watching her pink boots flash as she skipped alongside Laura. Rose's carefree steps brought every fear Rachel harbored to the fore. She would do *anything* to preserve Rose's happiness, to keep custody of her daughter.

"Kiss me, Rachel."

"What?" Rachel faced Shane, and the heat of the day seemed to press down upon her.

"Kiss me. And make sure the lawyer's watching."

*"Now?"* She couldn't kiss him now, Rachel thought dazedly, squinting against the glare of the sun. Cars were passing on the street. People walked the sidewalks.

Shane swept his arm about her waist. He pulled her close, the soft skirt of her dress catching on his jeans, his legs muscled and firm against her softer thighs. His knee crept between hers, and Rachel felt a welling of need inside her that pushed the air from her lungs.

Shane raised her against him and Rachel reached her hands to the back of his neck. His skin was hot, his thick hair silky. His hat brim shaded her from the sun, giving her a clear view of Shane's vibrant eyes, of his determined jaw as he whispered, "Now."

All the longing she'd stored for Shane speared through Rachel, and without another thought for the world carrying on around them, she met his kiss with a desperate hunger.

Shane responded with a desperation of his own. The kiss was hot, it was sweet; and when it was over, nei-

ther of them remembered to see if Howard Latham
was looking out the tack-shop window.

Evening found Rachel restless. When they'd returned from town, she'd changed from her dress to her
jeans to feed the horses and tidy up the barn. Now she
lingered near the barn door, listening to Rose play with
the kitten in its box. Outside, Shane and Laura stood
at the pasture fence after turning out Cash for a cool
evening run.

Instead the horse dropped and churned in the sand-
and-dirt mixture, sending dust clouds swirling against
a pink and blue skyline. Laura gave a snort of disgust. "So much for brushing him."

"Pretty don't win at calf roping," Shane said.

Rachel could hear the grin in Shane's voice and she
smiled over the truth of it. Some horses had a natural
shine but no talent, while others, whom no amount of
brushing could put a gloss on, had championship po-
tential. Cash was one of the latter, and he looked in his
element with dust covering his rugged brown coat.

"Grandma says, 'Pretty is as pretty does,'" Laura
recited. "Rachel's pretty, isn't she, Dad?"

Rachel brushed chaff from her shirtfront and curled
her hand near her heart, which all but stilled as she
awaited Shane's answer.

"Yes, she is," Shane said simply. "Not just on the
outside, but on the inside, where it counts."

"Just like Grandma meant," Laura said.

Rachel's heart softened and it had been a long time since she'd felt so warm inside—or so pretty on the outside. A real miracle, considering she was dressed in work jeans and boots.

"That was some kiss you gave Rachel today."

At Laura's words, Rachel's jaw went slack. Laura must have seen her and Shane out the window of the ice-cream parlor. And Laura clearly wanted an explanation.

Shane didn't miss a beat. "Yes, it was."

At his words, restlessness stirred within Rachel again.

"Did you kiss her because that man was watching? Or because she's so pretty?"

Laura had climbed up a rung on the fence and she hung her arm over the top board, looking Shane straight in the eye. Rachel wanted to look in his eyes, as well, to see his answer.

Shane didn't flinch from his daughter. "I'd have to say both. I guess it started because the man was watching, but all I was thinking about while it was going on was how pretty Rachel was."

Rachel closed her eyes, a sweet ache coming over her with his words even as she worried about the effect those words might have on Laura.

"I'm glad it was... real." Laura's voice dipped quietly. "Did you ever kiss Mom that way?"

Rachel unconsciously braced herself.

"I kissed her in a way that was special to us."

"So you *really* loved Mom."

"When we married, I really loved her." Shane rested his hand on Laura's shoulder. "And I'm sorry things didn't work out, that we couldn't remain a family."

"I love you, Dad." Laura tipped her head to rest her cheek on his hand.

The picture they made glistened and Rachel stored it in her heart. Shane's claim to have loved Lana and his regret over his failed marriage somehow reassured her, sent that ever-present hope within her spiraling to the sky. Rachel recalled the words Shane had once spoken, how he'd said he only hung around Oklahoma for Laura's sake. A question rose with the hope within her: why couldn't Shane stay for her and Rose, too?

# Chapter Nine

Shane rested his head against the back of Rachel's porch swing and shoved his hat down over his eyes. He stretched out his legs and crossed one boot over the other. When he'd wandered over, Rachel had just put Rose down for a nap and she and Laura had made themselves comfortable on the steps to talk. But that talk had fast shifted from horses to clothes and as they sat discussing hemlines, Shane's thoughts drifted to Rachel in her blue-flowered dress. It was a nice thought to doze off to.

Instead he listened to the feminine chatter, thinking Rachel and Laura not only looked like teenagers, but sounded like teenagers. They were weighing the merits of pierced ears now, and Rachel confided—

undoubtedly for his benefit—that she'd had her ears pierced at age thirteen.

Shane raised his eyelids a fraction. Rachel had showered after noon chores and she was wearing her tiny silver horseshoe earrings now, along with her white ruffled shirt. Her hair spilled over her bare smooth arms. Shane wasn't sure whether or not he'd let Laura get pierced earrings, but he thought he just might have to take the ladies into town for ice cream later.

He thought too, how Laura seemed to have struck up more of a friendship with Rachel than the mother-daughter relationship he'd feared. He should have been relieved, but he was uneasy, for a girl had to have a strong motherly influence; and in Laura's case that left only Emma....

"Dad, do you still have that ring your mother gave you?"

Shane pushed back his hat. Now he was truly awake and twice as uneasy. "The diamond?"

"Yes. The engagement ring."

Shane knew where this conversation was headed. Yet he sat gently rocking the swing, waiting and watching Rachel, who'd gone quiet.

"If Rachel was to wear the ring," Laura went on, "it would help convince people the engagement is real—like that man at the tack shop."

"That's a good idea," Rachel said quickly, "but it wouldn't be appropriate for me to wear Shane's mother's ring. That ring was probably special to her."

Rachel looked to him for confirmation then, and Shane nodded. "It was special. She and my father loved one another very much."

"I guess it wouldn't be right, then." Laura's sigh was wistful and Shane knew her disappointment ran deeper than was warranted. Laura might not see Rachel as a replacement for her mother, but it was clear she had no problem picturing Rachel wearing that ring and standing by her father's side.

Laura rose from the step. "Have you got any sugar, Dad? Tequila loves sugar."

Shane pulled some cubes from his pocket. Laura took them and walked toward the barn, popping a cube in her mouth as she did. Shane caught Rachel's tender smile as she watched his daughter.

"Thanks for helping set Laura straight. Sometimes she doesn't stop to think things through."

Rachel's smile was wry. "We're all guilty of that."

"Yes, we are." Even as they spoke, he imagined kissing Rachel's curving lips with no thought to the consequences. Lately, when he did stop to think about himself and Rachel, the only consequences were good ones, especially where the girls were concerned. "Years ago, I offered that ring to Lana. She favored a flashier setting. I guess I should have taken that as a sign."

Rachel said softly, "Jace once gave me a fancy diamond necklace for my birthday. It was real pretty. But all I'd asked was that he spend some time with me. I guess that was when I realized he didn't have anything more to offer.'' Rachel smiled through the pain and regret. "I didn't want anything from Jace after the divorce but that necklace. I'm saving that diamond for Rose.''

"You never wear it?''

"No. When I look at it, all I think is how it will help put Rose through college. When she's twenty-five, she'll have her trust fund.''

"At least you know Rose won't want for anything.''

"And I want *her* to know money can't buy everything. It's nice you still have your mother's ring to show Laura that love can be special. That it can be real.''

Rachel's gaze drifted out over the pasture and Shane's nostrils flared on an indrawn breath. Did she imagine what it would be like if their engagement was real, if he was to place that ring on her finger? God knew, he imagined it. He saw himself sharing in her and Rose's lives; saw them sharing in his and Laura's. The feelings swept over him like a much-needed rain, warming him like sun breaking through clouds. He knew, with a sudden sureness, that he wanted to reach out to Rachel, to go sit by her side and spend all the time with her that Jace hadn't wanted.

But Shane stayed in the swing. Jace still had a hold on Rachel. A hold he knew kept her from trusting her feelings; kept her from trusting in *him*. He could change that—with time.

Beneath the cast, Shane flexed his healing hand and arm. Then he set the swing slowly rocking.

Rachel took red ribbon from Rose's trinket box and awkwardly formed a tiny bow for Rose's yellow-haired doll. Rose sat on the bathroom counter before her, leaning close and smelling of baby shampoo. When both Rose and the doll had their ponytails properly adorned, Rose smiled at their images in the bathroom mirror.

Rachel lifted down Rose and the doll, and Rose caught her mother's legs and hugged tightly. Rachel reached to hug back, but Rose let go and ran from the room, out to watch from the door for Jace's wife, Elizabeth.

The empty feeling that ran through Rachel hurt and scared her. She wanted to call Rose back.

But Rose was excited about spending Sunday at Jace's big house, excited about Elizabeth coming for her this time.

Rachel didn't want to instill her fears in her daughter.

"Mommy! Mommy! It's 'Lizabeth."

Rose's excitement was tinged with uncertainty now. She wanted to go with Elizabeth, but she wanted her mother there to send her off, to reassure her. Rose didn't understand how much she was asking.

Pushing her hair past her shoulders, Rachel walked through the house, curling her hands in the pockets of her denim dress.

Rose waited at the door, her little nose pressed to the screen, her doll clutched close. "Mommy! 'Lizabeth is here!"

Rose turned then and saw her, and ran over for another hug. Rachel knelt and cuddled Rose close. Then she busily straightened Rose's denim jumper and the red ruffled shirt underneath. She tightened the laces on Rose's red tennis shoes. One last adjustment to the matching ruffled socks and Rose was ready. Rachel knew she never would be.

Rose pulled her out the door. Outside, the ranch was Sunday-morning quiet, hot-summer-day still. Elizabeth climbed from Jace's luxury sedan and Rose ran to greet her, their happy voices disturbing the silence and breaking Rachel's heart.

Somehow this was more difficult than when she sent Rose off with Jace. Rachel pressed her fingers to her lips while Elizabeth talked to Rose, touching Rose's ribboned ponytail and admiring the yellow-haired doll. When Rose took hold of Elizabeth's hand, Rachel thought she had never felt so alone.

Rachel blinked, lifting her gaze skyward, and saw Shane standing before the barn. Waiting. With one sign, she knew he would be by her side. Drawing a breath, Rachel stepped from the porch.

Elizabeth sent Rose skipping Shane's way. Rachel waited at the bottom of the porch steps while Elizabeth crossed the sunbaked yard.

Elizabeth's frosted blond hair was twisted at her nape in an elegant bun. A silk blouse and trousers draped her slender figure and she wore fine leather shoes on her feet. She didn't look her forty-plus years, Rachel thought, and she didn't look like the type a child could spill fruit punch on. She didn't look like a mother.

Rachel pushed her hands in her pockets. Belligerence and fear knotted her stomach. When Elizabeth reached her Rachel said, "Rose should be home by bedtime."

"I'll be sure to have her back." Elizabeth found herself caught between Rachel's tearful angry gaze and the warning glare of the young cowboy at the barn. Even now, he was gathering up Rose and heading this way, to the rescue. "I'll take good care of Rose," Elizabeth promised.

Rachel's face all but crumpled then and Elizabeth glanced away. "I've enjoyed the times I've spent with Rose. And I believe Jace is finally coming to realize how special his firstborn is to him. I know my first child was special to me. She always will be."

Rachel looked at her sharply. Elizabeth didn't look back, staring across the way at Shane and Rose approaching. "I was sixteen when my daughter was born. My parents—everyone—pressured me to give my baby away. And I did."

Rachel clenched her hands. *That doesn't mean you can have my baby....*

"It was a decision I have regretted with each passing day of my life." Elizabeth faced her then, and for the first time, Rachel saw the age in Elizabeth's blue eyes. "A baby belongs with its mother."

The words flowed over Rachel, breaching the wall around her. *A baby belongs with its mother....*

"My chances of getting pregnant and carrying my baby to term are slim," Elizabeth said with a composure Rachel now suspected hid a turmoil of emotion. "But no matter the outcome, I promise you Jace has agreed we will not seek custody of Rose."

Rachel's palms were sweaty, her heart beating hard. *We will not seek custody.... Jace agreed.... I promise....*

And in that moment Rachel realized that it was Elizabeth she'd feared more than Jace, despite his never-ending threats....

"Jace has regrets, too, Rachel," Elizabeth said astutely. "You left him before his child was born." A wry smile touched Elizabeth's face. "He's never known quite how to handle the situation—or you. But I can assure you now, that he does. We want only to know and to love Rose."

Shane had stopped a short distance away, listening. Now he set down Rose and Elizabeth turned to take hold of Rose's hand.

"Wait!" Rachel wiped her palms on her dress. She took the few steps to her daughter and lifted her, holding her tightly. Over the top of Rose's head, she met Elizabeth's gaze. "Be a good girl for Elizabeth," she whispered. "And for your daddy."

"I'll be good," Rose whispered back.

Rachel set down her daughter and let her go. The weight of her fear no longer rested heavily on her chest. The pain in her heart had eased.

But when Shane held out his hand, Rachel reached for it blindly.

Shane held her until the sound of Jace's car faded in the distance until the tension she'd carried released itself in tears on his shirt. Shane didn't mind. Rachel was washing away the past, letting go.

Rachel brushed the back of her hand across each cheek. "I believe Jace may have met his match in Elizabeth."

"I know he was no match for you." Feeling her exhaustion as she leaned against him, Shane stroked his hand over Rachel's hair.

She grew very still. Shane could feel her pulling away even before she raised her head. He fought a flash of frustration. He knew Rachel had feelings for him; he'd seen it in her eyes, felt it in her kiss that day in Guthrie. But he let his hand slide away when she drew back.

"I think I'll go inside for a while."

Shane tucked his hand in his pocket. He had to give her time now. He wasn't going to rush her, wasn't going to bully her like Jace. "Go ahead. Laura and I will tend to the horses tonight."

"I— Thank you."

Rachel went into the house. Closed the door. Shane filled his lungs. The hurt Jace had caused her would fade and Rachel's feelings for *him* would come clear to her. He'd shown that he cared for her and Rose. Knew she cared about him and Laura. He needed only to wait for a sign that she was ready to trust these feelings they had for one another.

When he turned back to the barn, Laura was standing in the doorway, a currycomb in her hand and an anxious expression on her face. Shane started over, letting Laura know with his smile that Rose and Rachel were fine. She lifted the currycomb in response and disappeared into the barn.

She was brushing Tequila when Shane walked in.

"You're going to wear the hide right off that horse," Shane teased.

Laura gave only a fleeting smile. Gravely she asked, "Was Rachel crying?"

"She was, but not out of sadness, Laura. Jace isn't going to try and take Rose away anymore. He's agreed she belongs with Rachel."

Laura stopped brushing the horse then. "That must be hard for Jace if he really wanted Rose with him."

Shane knew what she was asking, knew what Laura needed to hear. She watched him so closely, Shane wondered how she couldn't see the hurt inside him. "Jace is doing what's best for Rose, the way a father should."

Laura went back to brushing the horse. Shane walked to the barn door and stood in the hot bright sun. He'd given her the freedom to choose without guilt. Now he selfishly wished Laura would choose him.

He prayed for the strength to handle it if she didn't.

The long summer days were deceptively endless. All too soon, three-quarters of Laura's visit was gone.

Rachel walked through the quiet house to the kitchen for a glass of water. She'd just finished evening chores and the girls were still playing by the barn. She drained half a glass, then held it to her hot forehead, closing her eyes. Through the open window she could hear Rose and Laura, and Rachel thought she could stand here forever, listening to her daughter laugh that way.

The sound of Shane's pickup returning from Guthrie drifted from the lane and Rachel lifted the curtain aside.

The girls greeted him excitedly. Shane climbed from the truck, wearing his good white shirt, the sleeves rolled to his elbows. He'd been to the doctor and his cast was gone. For a moment, Rachel's heart stilled. Slowly, she set down the glass.

Laura ran into the barn and returned with Shane's rope. Rachel could hear her begging Shane to twirl it. Rose chimed in and Shane laughed, taking the rope. He ran it through his hands, coiling it, and Rachel could almost sense his satisfaction with the familiar feel of his rope in his hands.

Shane pushed back his hat. He raised his right arm, twirling the loop he'd made, and with a flick of his wrist sent it sailing neatly over a fence post. Shane jerked the rope taut. Rachel could imagine him stepping down from his horse, running the length of the rope to throw and tie his calf in winning time.

Laura whistled her approval and Rachel heard Rose beg, "Do that more."

Rose always wanted "more" from Shane. He had never disappointed her. Not yet.

Laura retrieved the rope for Shane and he coiled it again. As he did, he looked at the house, to the window where Rachel stood. She could feel his wanting come to her on the hot summer air, could sense his frustration, like she could sense a storm on the horizon.

Rachel clenched her hands on the counter. She wanted to believe that Shane loved her as she'd come to love him. She wanted to believe that it wasn't only Laura that kept him here.

Rachel's heart beat heavily. She knew, deep within her, that Laura would return to Emma, who had been like a mother to the girl. Would Shane turn to her this time, or would he seek to banish his heartache riding bulls on the rodeo circuit?

She didn't know. And in her uncertainty, all those seeds of doubt about Shane took root and flourished. She'd been wrong about Jace, hurt by Jace. What if she'd misjudged Shane, as well? She couldn't risk her and Rose being hurt again. She couldn't take it....

Shane turned away then, twirled the loop and sent it sailing.

A short while later Rachel called Rose into the house so they could take their baths. Shane planned to cook hamburgers on the grill for supper and Rachel decided to bake cookies for dessert. Rose was in the midst of things, perched on a chair and picking chocolate chips out of the mixing bowl, when there came a knock on the screen door. It was Shane's knock, and Rachel called him into the kitchen.

"Looks like you ladies are busy." Shane leaned in the kitchen doorway, hitching his thumbs in his front jeans pockets. Rachel grew warm as he took in her bare feet, flowered sundress and loosely woven braid, still damp from the shower. "What kind of cookies are you making?"

"Chocolate chip." *Your favorite*. Rachel remembered the day he'd bought one for her. And looking at him, she thought, *Now he has two arms to hold me....*

Shane looked back for a long moment, then he said, "Laura and I thought we'd go get pizzas and bring them back for supper. You can ride along if you're not too busy with the baking."

"I want to go!"

Rose had both hands full of chocolate chips now. Rachel lifted her from the chair. She realized that soon there might only be her and Rose together at suppertime. Rachel kept her gaze fixed on the table. "I need to stay, to get these cookies baked."

Shane held out his arms for Rose, who went willingly. "I think you've helped your mama enough. I want you to come with me and Laura."

"Because I'm your little Rosebud." Rose pushed a chocolate chip into Shane's mouth.

"Because you're my little Rosebud," Shane said. And without another word, another glance, he walked out of the kitchen.

The front door banged shut. Rachel stood, her fingers curled into her skirt, her emotions swirling. She heard the truck doors slam, the engine start.

*Go with him.*

*Stay.*

*Go. Go...*

But she was afraid, and after a moment her choice faded along with the sound of the pickup's engine down the lane.

Rachel was still standing there when she heard a car pulling up outside. Dusting her hands on her skirt she went to the door. A blue sedan was parked by the Indian blanket. An elderly woman climbed from the car and started up the walk. Rachel smiled a little. The woman wore the same kind of flowered dresses Lilly had worn. Rose had loved them.

Then Rachel saw the resemblance and realized this woman must be the sister Lilly had spoken of. Slipping on the sandals she'd left by the door, Rachel pushed open the screen and went outside.

The woman was slight and spry as Lilly had been before the broken hip. She trotted up the steps and held out her hand. "I'm Bess, Lilly's sister from Guthrie. And you must be Rachel."

"Yes, I am." Rachel shook Bess's hand. "Won't you come inside?"

"Oh, no. I've only stopped for a minute, on my way back from town with Lilly's prescription. But I'll sit in that swing with you a moment."

They settled in the swing and Rachel learned that Lilly was mending well. But it would be some time before Lilly could baby-sit Rose again. Bess was here to offer her services in place of her sister.

While Bess expressed disappointment over Rose's absence, Rachel considered the offer. Her gaze drifted about the ranch, taking in the pink evening sky and the quiet. Cash hung his head over the pasture gate, waiting for someone to let him back in the barn. The thought crossed Rachel's mind that she would miss the lazy brown gelding if Shane should take him away....

Rachel's throat tightened. When Bess stopped chattering to catch a breath, Rachel told her, "I expect I'll need you after this weekend."

# Chapter Ten

The relentless sun broke the sky, bringing the Sunday dawn of Laura's departure. Rachel woke to find a sleepy Rose climbing onto her bed. Holding Rose close, she wanted to linger, to put off the day that promised only goodbyes and would have her daughter crying.

But the sun pushed on and morning chores awaited. After breakfast, Rachel took Rose to the barn. Laura and Shane were already there, Shane teasing his daughter as if this day were no different from any other. But his gaze was as dark as the sadness Rachel knew lay in his heart. Laura's smile lacked luster and reflected the dull ache Rachel felt within her.

Knowing Shane and Laura needed some time alone, Rachel eventually herded Rose toward the house, promising to play catch with her. Halfway there, Rose had a change of heart. Rachel convinced her to go sit on the porch, this time promising to fetch Rose's kitten from the barn to keep her company.

Rachel hurried, casting a watchful eye over her shoulder to make sure Rose waited on the step. Just inside the barn she halted, stopped by the sound of Laura crying.

"You know I love you, Dad."

Laura was in Tequila's stall, her dark head bowed. Rachel took a hesitant step back, not wanting to intrude, yet drawn painfully to listen.

"There's nothing you could do to make me doubt that, Laura," Shane assured her, his voice soft and low.

The myriad sounds of the morning couldn't fill the silence that followed. Rachel knew at what cost Shane's words had been spoken, but even she wasn't braced for the hurt that came with hearing Laura say, "I can't stay with you, Daddy."

Rachel pressed her hands to her lips. She could see Shane's broad shoulders hunch as he took the blow.

"I want to," Laura went on, her voice breaking. "But Grandpa hasn't been well. Grandma's worried and I can't just leave them— "

Laura was crying in earnest now and Shane put his arms around her. "Shh . . . You don't have to have excuses. It's reason enough that you love your grandma and grandpa."

"I do love them. And they love me. They need me."

And although Rachel knew Shane needed Laura, too, she heard him say, "I guess I can only be proud of the decision you've made."

"You always tell me to stop and think, and I did. Now all I can think is how I wish there were two of me, so I could stay with Grandma and Grandpa and still be here with you."

And Rachel heard Shane whisper, "I wish there were two of you, too."

Somehow, in the midst of drying her tears and retrieving the kitten, Rachel managed to slip from the barn unnoticed. Her heart ached for Laura, forced to choose between the people the girl so obviously loved. Then her heart broke, as she thought of Shane, knowing how he must hurt, knowing he might leave her now.

Rachel sat beside Rose with the kitten. Earlier, Rose had been playing rambunctiously in the barn. But now she was behaving too well, staying here on the step, as she'd been told. And her little face was too solemn. She kept watching the barn door for Shane and Laura.

Rachel had explained that Laura would likely be leaving today, and knew that was from where Rose's quiet stemmed. She didn't know what she would tell Rose if Shane left them, too. She knew better now that despite Shane's efforts to avoid any hurt, they would be affected by his leaving.

After a while, Rachel coaxed Rose inside to bake more cookies for Laura to take with her. She also made Laura's favorite fried chicken while the hands of the clock moved steadily on.

Evening slipped over the ranch, the day's breeze dying down, the purple sky seeming to still in the quiet. Rachel had let Rose skip a nap that day, and now Rose slept on her lap in the swing, lulled by the rocking, one hand curled trustingly in the skirt of Rachel's blue-flowered dress. Rachel thought how lucky she was to have her daughter to keep, safe in her arms.

Shane and Laura walked from the barn, Shane with his arm curved about Laura's shoulder, she with her arm wrapped around his waist. They slowed near the bottom of the porch steps, turning at the sound of a car in the lane.

Rachel straightened. She longed to go to Shane. But this was out of her hands. Rachel settled back in the swing with Rose. She could only be here for Shane, could only pray he would turn to her when it was over.

The Blackwells' Cadillac glided to a stop. Rachel saw Laura's hesitance, the girl obviously longing to see her grandparents, yet not wanting to hurt her father. Shane drew his arm from around her. "Run on down and greet them."

"Are you sure?" Laura clasped her hands before her, uncertain.

"You're doing the right thing, Laura." Shane gave her a gentle push. "Go on, now. They've missed you."

Laura dashed off. Rachel was only vaguely aware of the exchange of hugs at the car, her heart and soul drawn to Shane. He rocked his weight tiredly to one boot, his arms hanging, his hands curled as if to hold all the hurt inside. The brim of his hat rose with the lift of his chin when Emma came up the walk, leaving Laura and Gus to head for the barn.

Rose stirred, and Rachel loosened the hold she'd taken on her daughter. She ought to leave Shane and Emma alone. But Emma didn't hesitate in her presence, and Rachel murmured soothingly to Rose, staying seated. If there was any chance Shane would turn to her, she wanted to be near him.

"Laura seems to have had a wonderful visit," Emma said graciously. But Rachel recognized Emma's relief that Laura's time here hadn't stolen her granddaughter away.

Rachel could sympathize with Emma even as her heart slowly broke for Shane.

"Yes, she did," Shane said simply. Quietly. As if the dream he'd carried for years hadn't ended unfulfilled.

Laura and Gus emerged from the barn. Emma said quickly, "Gus took Laura aside so that I might tell you you're welcome to see Laura any time, regardless of her mother's wishes." Emma's voice wavered. "Looking back, we regret ever having taken—"

"Looking back doesn't do any of us good now," Shane pointed out. "Especially Laura."

"No." Emma straightened. "It doesn't."

They regarded one another, each loving Laura, each needing to put aside the past to do what was best for her now.

But seeing Shane's hands clench, his gaze riveted on his daughter, Rachel thought in that moment that it might be beyond Shane to do so. Then he said, "I'll come see Laura often."

Emma nodded. "Gus and I will let you say your goodbyes."

Emma called to Laura, then returned to the car to wait with Gus. Laura came onto the porch and knelt by Rose, who still dozed. "Should I wake her?" Laura whispered.

She clearly wanted to. Rachel smiled and gently shook Rose's shoulder. "Rose, it's time to say good-bye to Laura."

Rose's eyes opened. Then closed. And opened again. She smiled at Laura's face close to hers.

"Grandpa says you can come visit me at his house," Laura told Rose. "Would you like that?"

"I would like that." Rose blinked sleepily.

Laura kissed Rose's forehead. "Bye, Rose. See you soon."

"See you soon," Rose echoed, her eyes already closed, the smile still on her face.

Rachel suspected the tears would come later. She reached out and hugged Laura, saving her tears for later, too.

"I'd better go now." Laura had whispered again, and her eyes were uncertain.

Rachel repeated the words Laura needed to hear. "You're doing the right thing."

After one last hug, Laura went to Shane and flung her arms about him. He held her tightly. Rachel held Rose, feeling helpless beyond her silent prayer.

Laura let go of her father and ran to the car, climbing in. She waved once as the car circled and headed down the lane. Shane waved back.

Rachel saw his jaw tighten. She'd been rocking Rose; now she let the swing still. Shane's chest heaved on an indrawn breath. Rachel slid from beneath her daughter, settling Rose on the quilt she'd laid over the seat. Shane drew his raised hand to his eyes and she went down the porch steps.

Shane pressed his lips, but the tears he willed away burned hotly as the moment branded itself in his mind.

This time, the pain of Laura's decision outweighed any remaining resentment he might have had for Gus and Emma. He didn't want an angry bull to ride. This time he wanted, needed, the understanding Rachel would offer. He would hold her, and he would never let go....

Shane felt Rachel's warmth beside him. He would have reached for her then, but the sound of a car door opening stopped him. A blue sedan had come down the lane unnoticed. An elderly woman climbed from the car and Shane scrubbed his hand down his face at the intrusion.

Rachel had gone still beside him, but when the woman started up the walk she hurried forward. They met halfway and their words hung heavily in the warm evening air.

"I was just driving by and wanted to check with you about baby-sitting Rose," the woman said, her cheery tone fading as she realized she'd come at an awkward time. "Did you still want me to come tomorrow?"

"I—I'm not sure." Rachel guided the woman back toward the car.

Disbelief wound through Shane's misery. Rachel expected him to leave her. Despite all he'd done to show her he loved her, she envisioned him walking away from her and Rose, now that his daughter had gone....

Shane swore under his breath, his heart pounding furiously as fresh hurt set in and anger gripped him. Rachel spoke earnestly to the woman, who nodded. Shane spun away and strode to his truck.

Climbing in, Shane slammed the door and wheeled the truck near the barn to hitch up his horse trailer. He stowed his tack, then led out Cash and loaded him, aware that the blue car had started down the lane. Rachel was heading his way. He'd secured the trailer door when she caught his arm.

"Shane, you don't understand."

At her touch, all the pain seemed to well within him. Laura was gone. And if Rachel didn't trust in his love, there seemed to be nothing to hold him here now....

Shane jerked his arm from her grasp. "I understand you'll never be free of Jace. You're so damned afraid of making a mistake because things didn't work out with him. Well, lady, you just made a mistake about me."

Shane shoved down his hat and turned away. He yanked open the truck door and got in, heading his rig down the lane. He didn't look back.

Dust formed a red haze in the sun's last rays. Numb, Rachel returned to the porch, kneeling to sit beside Rose, who slept on in the swing. She smoothed her daughter's fair hair and thought of the man who had helped create Rose. She no longer feared Jace might take Rose away. But Shane was right. As long as she was afraid to love again, she wouldn't be free of Jace.

Rachel closed her eyes. That knowledge had come too late. Shane was gone. She doubted he'd return for what little he'd left in the trailer. More likely, he would just keep going, for she'd given him no reason to come back.

Tiny fingers flickered her eyelashes. "Wake up, Mommy."

Rachel opened her eyes. Rose lay with her head on the quilt, sleepy and warm.

"Where is Laura?"

"She went home," Rachel gently reminded. "To her grandma and grandpa's house."

"I can come visit," Rose quoted.

"Yes, you can." Rachel breathed a sigh of relief. If Rose had started crying now, she'd have joined in and never stopped.

"Where is Shane?" Rose sat up, blinking and looking about the quiet ranch. Rachel thought she might cry anyway as she again pictured Shane tossing his gear in the truck, loading Cash. She recalled his anger, but even more, she remembered the hurt she'd seen in his eyes; hurt she was in part responsible for.

Rachel got up and sat in the swing beside Rose. "Do you remember Shane telling how he likes to ride in the rodeo?"

Rose snuggled close. "So Cash can win prizes. He likes to win prizes. Then Shane gives him sugar."

"Well, Shane had to leave. He took Cash, so he might go to the rodeo. He might be gone a long time."

"He'll bring me presents when he comes back."

"Did Shane say that?"

Rose's head bobbed with the sureness of each word as she recited, "Because I'm his little Rosebud. And he'll think of us last thing at night."

*Think of us...* Rachel hugged Rose tight. Shane had kept his promise not to hurt Rose. And he'd shown, time and again, that he wouldn't hurt *her*. She'd wound up hurting him instead, never trusting the love that was right before her eyes.

Rachel set the swing in motion, holding Rose, and rocked her daughter to sleep. The breeze came up to cool them and a million stars filled the sky.

Regret weighed heavily in Rachel's heart. She thought of Rose's faith in Shane's return; a faith based on love. She realized that if she believed in Shane's love, she, too, had to believe he would be back. She would wait here each night, she promised herself, until Shane returned.

A single star fell, and Rachel made a fervent wish.
And she prayed that wherever Shane was, he thought
of them last thing this night.

Shane fumbled with the gate latch, then gave Cash
a slap on the rump to get the reluctant horse on
through to the pasture. Cash might want a freshly
bedded stall and a full hay bag, but Shane had spent a
long night and day gone from the ranch. Now, by
moonlight, he was back, and he wasn't going to let a
second night go by without making things clear to
Rachel.

Latching the gate, Shane walked toward the house,
careful not to tramp on the Indian blanket. When he
reached the porch he slowed, catching sight of Rachel
sleeping in the swing.

His boots scraped the porch floor despite his best
efforts and Shane wondered how Rachel didn't waken.
She was curled on the swing like a child and he sat
close, feeling the warmth of her through her pink
nightshirt and his jeans. Her long, lowered lashes entranced him. And the sweep of her gold hair over the
cotton that covered her breasts reminded him of the
time he'd kissed her here in the swing. Shane touched
Rachel's cheek, waking her, hoping he would be welcome.

Rachel woke slowly, and a soft warm look came into
her eyes, as if she'd been waiting here just for him. "I
knew you'd come back."

"I never should have left. I should have stayed and said the things you needed to hear."

Rachel pressed her fingers to his lips. "I love you, Shane. And I know you love me."

Pleasure washed over him with her words. "I guess I needed to hear it, too."

Rachel scooted up on the seat. "You look tired."

"I've been clear to northern Nebraska and back." Shane swept off his hat and dropped it to the porch floor. He wanted to do this right. He dug into the pocket of his white shirt and pulled out a ring. He took Rachel's small hand in his. "This is my mother's ring. I love you Rachel. And I'm asking you to marry me."

He slipped the ring on her finger and the tiny facets caught the starlight and glittered.

Rachel touched Shane's shadowed jaw. His eyes were dark from lack of sleep and the hurt he'd suffered. "We could live here, Shane, where you can be near Laura. And when you rodeo, Rose and I will always be here to come home to."

"If I rodeo, you and Rose will come with me. Laura, too, whenever she can. But, more and more, I see myself staying right here on the ranch, training roping horses—" Shane grinned now "—after you've schooled them in the basics, of course."

"That sounds real nice."

Rachel smiled. But Shane was suddenly solemn. "I'll be a good father to Rose. And I'll be a good husband to you, Rachel. I'll never take for granted what you feel, what you need, what you want."

Rachel wrapped her arms around Shane's neck. "I want you to kiss me."

And so he did. Then he took her down in the swing and let his hand rest warmly on her belly. "I hope we'll need that baby-sitter, after all," he whispered.

"I hope so, too."

And Rachel made a fervent wish on the stars shining down, knowing she had found lasting love in the arms of the real Shane Purcell.

*     *     *     *     *

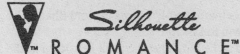

# Silhouette ROMANCE™

# COMING NEXT MONTH

**#1150  WELCOME HOME, DADDY!—Kristin Morgan**
*Fabulous Fathers*
The Murdock marriage was over—or was it? Ross Murdock was determined to win back his wife, Rachel, especially after discovering another baby was on the way!

**#1151  AN UNEXPECTED DELIVERY—Laurie Paige**
*Bundles of Joy*
Talk about labor pains! Any-minute-mom-to-be Stacey Gardenas was on an assignment when her baby decided to be born. And that meant her handsome boss, Gareth Clelland, had to help deliver the child.

**#1152  AN IMPROMPTU PROPOSAL—Carla Cassidy**
*The Baker Brood*
Colleen Jensen was desperate—and Gideon Graves was the only one who could help her. But while searching for Colleen's missing brother, would Gideon find the way to her heart?

**#1153  THE RANCHER AND THE LOST BRIDE—
Carol Grace**
Parker's sweet little girl made Christine feel like part of the family—as did the sparks between her and the rugged rancher!
But could forgotten memories keep Christine from being a *true* family member?

**#1154  AND MOMMY MAKES THREE—Lynn Bulock**
Long ago, Matt Viviano gave up on love and happy endings. But the way Larissa Camden lit up his son's face was a dream come true, and if Matt wasn't careful, he'd find himself in his own storybook romance.

**#1155  FAMILY MINE—Elizabeth Krueger**
Marriage? Meredith Blackmoore refused to even *consider* marrying Stoney Macreay. She could not ignore her daughter's wish for a father and Stoney's desire for a family, but could she resist *her* own need for Stoney?

# As seen on TV!
## *Free Gift Offer*

With a Free Gift proof-of-purchase from any Silhouette® book,
you can receive a beautiful cubic zirconia pendant.

This gorgeous marquise-shaped stone is a genuine cubic
zirconia—accented by an 18" gold tone necklace.
(Approximate retail value $19.95)

## Send for yours today...
compliments of  *Silhouette*®

To receive your free gift, a cubic zirconia pendant, send us one original proof-of-purchase, photocopies not accepted, from the back of any Silhouette Romance™, Silhouette Desire®, Silhouette Special Edition®, Silhouette Intimate Moments® or Silhouette Shadows™ title available in February, March or April at your favorite retail outlet, together with the Free Gift Certificate, plus a check or money order for $1.75 U.S./$2.25 CAN. (do not send cash) to cover postage and handling, payable to Silhouette Free Gift Offer. We will send you the specified gift. Allow 6 to 8 weeks for delivery. Offer good until April 30, 1996 or while quantities last. Offer valid in the U.S. and Canada only.

## *Free Gift Certificate*

Name: _____

Address: _____

City: _____ State/Province: _____ Zip/Postal Code: _____

Mail this certificate, one proof-of-purchase and a check or money order for postage and handling to: SILHOUETTE FREE GIFT OFFER 1996. In the U.S.: 3010 Walden Avenue, P.O. Box 9057, Buffalo NY 14269-9057. In Canada: P.O. Box 622, Fort Erie,

---

**FREE GIFT OFFER**  079-KBZ-R
ONE PROOF-OF-PURCHASE
To collect your fabulous FREE GIFT, a cubic zirconia pendant, you must include this original proof-of-purchase for each gift with the properly completed Free Gift Certificate.

---

079-KBZ-R

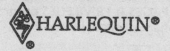

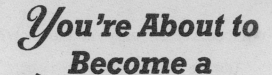